BOUND

THE HOUSE OF CRIMSON & CLOVER VOLUME IV

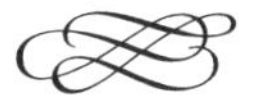

SARAH M. CRADIT

Cover Design by Sarah M. Cradit
Editing by Shaner Media Creations

First Edition
ISBN-10: 1505561507
ISBN-13: 978-1505561500

Publisher Contact:
sarah@sarahmcradit.com
www.sarahmcradit.com

FOREWORD

The House of Crimson & Clover continues here in the fourth book, *Bound,* and with it, the world is colored in with details that will matter as the story progresses into subsequent books.

Do you believe in fated love? I do. I believe it's rare, but real, and this particular installment in the series was written with that belief at heart.

Some readers have requested family trees, and you can find these on my website: sarahmcradit.com. There's also a substantial amount of bonus material that enhances the reading experience, even beyond what you can find in the books. This includes encyclopedias of people and places, which you may find useful later in the series especially.

Lastly, if you're reading this, this version is a re-edit—and you might recognize this note from the prior books, if you read them in their re-edited versions, too. Much like when Stephen King tackled his own re-edit of *The Gunslinger,* when you've been writing in a world for a long time, sometimes things change. Most of the edits are cosmetic. Some are small details that make later reconciliations in the series (and other series, like The Seven) smoother. If you've read the original version, and now this one, though, you'll hopefully notice no changes aside from readability. The story is the same. The characters, still the characters. The outcomes, and the tragic consequences, no different.

ALSO BY SARAH M. CRADIT

THE SAGA OF CRIMSON & CLOVER

The House of Crimson and Clover Series

The Storm and the Darkness

Shattered

The Illusions of Eventide

Bound

Midnight Dynasty

Asunder

Empire of Shadows

Myths of Midwinter

The Hinterland Veil

The Secrets Amongst the Cypress

Within the Garden of Twilight

House of Dusk, House of Dawn

Midnight Dynasty Series

A Tempest of Discovery

A Storm of Revelations

The Seven Series

1970

1972

1973

1974

1975

1976

1980

Vampires of the Merovingi Series

The Island

Crimson & Clover Lagniappes (Bonus Stories)

Lagniappes are standalone stories that can be read in any order.

St. Charles at Dusk: The Story of Oz and Adrienne

Flourish: The Story of Anne Fontaine

Surrender: The Story of Oz and Ana

Shame: The Story of Jonathan St. Andrews

Fire & Ice: The Story of Remy & Fleur

Dark Blessing: The Landry Triplets

Pandora's Box: The Story of Jasper & Pandora

The Menagerie: Oriana's Den of Iniquities

A Band of Heather: The Story of Colleen and Noah

The Ephemeral: The Story of Autumn & Gabriel

Banshee: The Story of Giselle Deschanel

For more information, and exciting bonus material, visit www.

sarahmcradit.com

"He felt now that he was not simply close to her, but that he did not know where he ended and she began."

Leo Tolstoy

1- NICOLAS

Nicolas Deschanel had never been a fan of these types of meetings. Or meetings at all, for that matter.

Outside the offices of Sullivan & Associates, the sun was setting over New Orleans' Central Business District. Inside, exhaustion had turned to frustration, as the lawyers and Deschanels continued their verbal tug-of-war for nearly six hours.

Nicolas would periodically lose focus, his thoughts wandering to the unimportant artifacts surrounding him. The long, oval mahogany table sparkled with the scent of almond-oil furniture polish. A silver tray in the middle, housing the day's refreshments, testified to the day's mind-numbing nature. The biscotti had grown drier, and the ice in the cut-crystal carafe had long-since melted. Condensation pooled atop the tray.

It had been a tedious afternoon. He'd loosened his ridiculous tie hours ago, ignoring the glares from Aunt Colleen when the buttons on his shirt also eventually came undone. But as primary heir to the Deschanel estate, he had no choice but to continue suffering through the discussions.

On one side of the table, the Sullivan attorneys most familiar with the Deschanel estate: Colin Sullivan and his brother, Rory.

On the other side, the Deschanels who had a vested interest in the matter: Nicolas, his aunts Colleen and Evangeline, and his uncle, Augustus.

Initially, Nicolas had been offended when Aunt Colleen insisted on bringing in the cavalry. Was he not capable of handling this on his own? But after slogging through hours of dry debate, he decided he was grateful for her intervention. They knew far more about the nuances of the estate. If this had been left up to him, he'd have told everyone to go fuck themselves, and named Ana's unborn son as heir, regardless of their objections. Bastard or no.

"The Deschanel will has been inviolate for almost two hundred years," Colin had rebutted at least a dozen times. He kept saying it whenever an objection was made, as if repetition would put a finer point on the mantra.

"I'm the heir, correct?" Nicolas would rhetorically ask. After their nods, "And you're my attorneys?" which earned him additional agreement. "So just change it for me!"

They'd then exchange looks. Nicolas didn't need to employ his newfound telepathy to read their minds. He was, clearly, not getting it.

But Nicolas *did* get it. He was well aware of how his ancestors had set up the Deschanel will, with very specific codicils, and rules, and other outdated legal garbage. The family had always followed those regulations, without quarrel. He understood the estate passed to the eldest son, through each generation. That, in the absence of a son, a daughter could inherit, so long as *her* son bore the name Deschanel.

Nicolas was never going to have children. He had no interest in following his father's piss poor example and, conveniently, his partner, Mercy, was barren. Nicolas' younger sister, Adrienne, wanted nothing to do with the estate. Anne, his other sister, was the product of an undocumented affair and no amount of negotiation would make the legal team comfortable with her descent being considered—and in any case, she didn't want it any more than Adrienne.

So Nicolas had chosen Anasofiya, his first cousin and dearest friend, as his heir. When Ana learned she was having a child, she asked Nicolas to make her son, Aleksandr, the heir immediately, instead of waiting until he reached maturity.

Filing that paperwork had launched the meeting to end all meetings. They'd tediously worked through most of the concerns presented, but the biggest one lingered: Ana wasn't married. Her child, then, would be born illegitimate.

"This is the 21st century! Who the fuck cares?" Nicolas exclaimed, to a crowd of stoic faces. They were acclimated to his unfiltered outbursts now, so it was impossible to draw a reaction from them.

"Nicolas, I realize this seems archaic to you, but abiding by these rules has been the solitary thread holding this family together," Aunt Colleen explained, in soothing tones which he found incredibly condescending despite his affection for the family matriarch. In her tan linen suit, crisp blouse, and manicured nails, she could have sat on either side of the table.

"Yes, because we're all such a happy, tight-knit bunch," Nicolas said, with biting sarcasm. "Thank God for all this ancient paper."

"Family dynamics aside," Colin interjected, "no one has ever contested your right to be the heir. Or your father's. Or his father's."

Nicolas' other aunt, Evangeline, cleared her throat. Evangeline was a stark contrast to her older sister, Colleen: long, loose hair, no makeup. Her eyes, as always, had a wild, exotic look to them. Evangeline, the scientist, looked every bit the eccentric brainiac. "This family has survived for centuries, as strong as it has, because we honor traditions. Without them, we would have no structure, no cohesion. Why, our Broussard cousins have been arguing for *years* the estate should be divided equally, and there should not even be an heir—"

"Fuck the Broussards!"

"Language," Colleen admonished.

"Whose side are you two on, anyway?" Nicolas snapped.

Colleen wrapped her thin fingers around Nicolas' hand. He moved to pull away, but she tightened her grip, and sent him these thoughts: *I'm on your side, nephew. Always. There are some battles you can't win. This is one of them. We will make this work. I promise.*

Nicolas kept his steely glare, but relaxed slightly. "So, what then? I have to choose someone else? Because that's not an option."

"Ana needs to marry the father of her child," Rory Sullivan asserted. He then added, wrinkling his nose, "Or, if she doesn't *know* who the father is—"

"She's not a whore, Rory," Nicolas defended, through gritted teeth. "Finn St. Andrews is the father, and he's ready and eager to play a role in his son's life."

At this, Augustus, Ana's estranged father, raised an eyebrow. He was here on her behalf, as she couldn't be, but the meeting had been full of displeasing revelations for the formidable businessman. A boardroom in a law office was not the best place to learn about things your only daughter had been up to.

"Nicolas, as your lawyers, we're advising you this child-heir needs to be born in wedlock, and there needs to be no dispute over who his parents are. Is there a reason Ana isn't willing to marry Finn?" Colin inquired, with an affected tone of reasonableness.

"Because she shouldn't have to? Because this isn't the fucking Middle Ages?" Nicolas bitterly retorted, followed by one of his favorite obscene hand gestures. The day, though, had worn him down. When even his two aunts—whom he respected a great deal—were defending the attorneys' stance, he knew it was time to stop being difficult, and start preparing.

"I still fail to understand why Ana cannot be here to speak for herself. No one has offered a single adequate explanation on the matter," Augustus complained gruffly. Nicolas almost felt bad for his uncle. The man truly loved his daughter but had never really understood Ana, instead choosing to ignore the unpleasant, or anything which didn't fit his orderly vision of the world.

No one answered his question. The Sullivans didn't know the answer, and Nicolas and his aunts were sworn to secrecy. But there was a very good reason Ana wasn't present to speak for herself. The same reason she was in hiding, and would stay that way, until it was safe to do otherwise.

Anasofiya Deschanel was no longer entirely human. And her unborn son, Aleksandr, would be born full Empyrean. Within weeks of birth, he'd stand as tall as his two fathers.

Despite Ana being in the capable hands of one of the oldest, and most knowledgeable, of all Empyreans, her life, and that of her unborn son, were in grave danger.

NICOLAS JOINED HIS AUNTS FOR A LATE DINNER AT GALATOIRE'S, in the Quarter.

"I know today was frustrating for you, Darling," Evangeline empathized, after a long swallow of her sazerac. "I'm sorry if you felt ganged up on."

Nicolas exchanged a glance with Colleen, remembering the calming thought she'd sent him hours ago. "Apology accepted," he said, with unusual restraint.

"You know Colin and Rory are right. Don't you?" Colleen asked.

"No... I mean, yes, I get their point. But it's fucking dumb, and antediluvian. I just need that stated for the record."

"The record hereby denotes your sentiments," Evangeline acknowledged, raising her glass in the air. "And the record also notes we agree, and find this equally idiotic."

"But necessary," Colleen added firmly. She leaned in and lowered her voice, despite the restaurant being loud with chatter. "It has never been more important to protect the estate. Now that we know... all we know..."

Yes, Nicolas picked up what she was alluding to. The past months had been full of startling revelations about what it really meant to be a Deschanel. While most of the family had special abilities to some degree—telepathy, healing, telekinesis, among other things—no one had ever stopped to ask the ever-important question: *where the hell did it come from?* Last winter, they'd inadvertently come across the answer.

"So what do we do?" Nicolas asked. His rare deference was driven by exhaustion, but also fear. If they didn't solve this to the satisfaction of the family, there could be dire consequences. This wasn't about one of the other cousins getting butt-hurt and trying to steal his inheritance. They were all in very real danger.

"Go home tonight and speak with Finn," Colleen replied. "He may be more amenable to the arrangement than you might think. He is, after all, still very much in love with Ana, despite her leaving without him. And there's always money if sentiment isn't a selling point."

"It isn't Finn we'll need to convince," Nicolas asserted, staring at the glimmering Hennessy behind the bar, calling his name.

It's been a while, Nicolas. Are we gonna dance?

2- FINN

Finn spent the morning down at the riverbank. He wasn't overly fond of oily catfish, and the Mississippi River was no Atlantic Ocean, but it kept his mind busy. Productive activity prevented him from wandering down to a local bar in Vacherie, and engaging in the trouble of his youth. Giving into reckless inclinations was something the old Finn would have done. The carefree Finn who existed before Anasofiya Deschanel walked into his life, and turned it completely upside down.

Finn always rose before the sun. Having spent his entire twenty-seven years in Maine, and nearly half of those on the sea, it was an intrinsic part of who he was. The desire to be on the water hadn't changed with his temporary shift to Louisiana. He'd simply adapted to his new surroundings. And so, he would spend his mornings, and early afternoons, just beyond the levee across River Road. By the time he returned to the plantation, night owls Nicolas and Mercy would barely be getting out of bed.

Not today, though. When he brought his catch to the back door of *Ophélie* for Condoleezza to work her magic on, he learned Nicolas had already left for New Orleans. *Legal mumbo jumbo,* she explained, with a shake of the head which made it very clear she didn't know and didn't *want* to know.

Finn, of course, knew Nicolas' intent was to make his son the heir of *Ophélie,* and, by extension, the entire Deschanel estate. Nicolas made the decision not long after Ana took off with Aidrik, leaving Finn behind with far more questions than he would likely ever get satisfying answers for. Days before, though, he'd overheard conversations between Nicolas and Mercy indicating there were some legal problems with making Finn's son the heir.

No one had come to Finn directly about it. More than likely, they were afraid to.

Back home, the residents of Summer Island would have never accused Finn of being delicate, but it was probably exactly what his housemates in Louisiana thought of him these past few months. In Maine, he would have been laboring at the dock, or out on the sea, embracing the physical effort on which his business was built. Away from home, and having lost Ana, he had become a useless shell of his former self, without meaningful direction, or purpose.

But Nicolas and Mercy were wrong in their assumptions. Finn's seclusion wasn't sulking. He went down to the river because it was where he did his best thinking. Where he felt the most like himself, connected to his capacity for finding reason and bearing amid chaotic disappointment.

Finn found it easier to process his thoughts when he took an inventorial approach to them. Summarizing took out all the emotional messiness. It forced information into a position where data was clear and concise, and decisions could be made.

Broken down to its key elements, his assessment was remarkably simple: he loved Ana Deschanel. Finn had been with many women, and none ever produced a feeling in him like this. Going from indifference about the better sex, to this powerful drop-kick-me-into-the-ocean passion, was surprising, but that surprise didn't fill him with doubt. *When you know, you know,* his mother once said. And Finn knew.

Finn wasn't blind to Ana's problems. She'd spent her whole life believing she was functionally broken, when the truth was, she'd simply been surrounded by people who inadvertently encouraged this falsehood. She found it difficult to connect with others, but there was far more to Ana than her social inadequacies. Finn had seen her immeasurable kindness, and her selflessness that was subtle, but significant. And while it was her natural inclination to push people away, Finn offered Ana not only acceptance, but understanding. *You're my first safe place,* Finn had told her, back in Maine. *I feel the same,* she'd confessed, as astounded as he'd been to find this sensation in another.

A series of events, and revelations, entirely changed everyone's worlds. His, Ana's, Nicolas'. It would be easy for Finn to feel sorry for himself and pretend he was the only one hurting. But he knew better.

It would also be tempting for Finn to grossly oversimplify the matter and blame Mercy for the most recent string of life-altering proceedings. After all, if she hadn't come into Nicolas' life, then Aidrik wouldn't have shown up looking for her. And if Aidrik hadn't shown up, then Ana wouldn't have been given the Sveising, and become more Empyrean than human. Her life wouldn't be in danger. Their son would belong only to them, and not also to Aidrik.

But things were not that simple at all. Ana had been planning to leave Finn even before Aidrik came along. When Finn discovered her fleeing to New Orleans in secret, he followed, knowing it wasn't that she didn't want him so much as her need to inflict more punishment on herself. She'd attempted to take her own life, but Aidrik had saved her, when Finn could not. But in saving her, Aidrik changed her.

All Deschanels have some Empyrean blood. It's why we can read minds and move shit across the room, Nicolas explained later. *But because of the Sveising, Ana now has more Empyrean blood than human.*

What does that mean? Finn had asked. A seemingly fruitless endeavor as, no matter how many times it was explained to him, he never gained further clarity.

It means... shit, we don't know what it means. It means the abilities she had before Aidrik changed her are now amplified. She's stronger, for sure. Fuck, you saw her resurrect Mercy. Ana might even live forever, like Aidrik. We really don't know.

No one, not even the universally respected Aunt Colleen, seemed to know. It defied all rational explanation, and even Finn, with his vibrant imagination, couldn't begin to wrap his head around it. He'd stepped outside of the comfort of what he knew, and was now wading into waters unknown.

What he did know was this: Ana was pregnant with his child. His *son.* But when Aidrik saved her via the Sveising, it not only fused his own precious DNA to Ana, but also to Finn's son. Their son now had two fathers, not one.

Finn wanted to throw his head back and scream into the swampland. *No! You can't have* my *son! You can't have Ana!* But screaming wouldn't bring Ana back. She'd made her choice.

Everyone recommended Finn move on. He was perfectly within his right. Even Nicolas, who was more loyal to Ana than anyone, suggested Finn should start seeing other people.

But Finn wasn't a chump. Nor was he the lovesick fool others saw him to be when he'd followed her to New Orleans. No matter how many different times, or ways, Finn tried to rationalize walking away, he couldn't. As long as he lived, he would never forget the look in Ana's eyes as she walked away: anguish. Her heart broke to say the words, as much as his broke to hear them.

She's not leaving for herself. She's leaving for me. Ana is afraid for me, and loves me too much to put me in danger. And she's punishing herself, as she has always done, because she doesn't know any better. In her mind, Aidrik is broken and damaged too, and somehow this means they belong together. Ana doesn't believe she deserves me.

Finn's days by the river had given him a compassionate and broad insight. It allowed him to focus on what really mattered: Ana and their son.

It took four months to come to the conclusion he was pulled toward going to her. The more he considered this option, the more confident he became it was the right decision, if he could only figure out *how*. Ana needed to feel protective arms encircling her, enveloping her in kindness, and strength. *My Poseidon,* she'd once called him, a moniker originally bestowed upon Finn by his mother.

Somewhere, Anasofiya was sleeping, and dreaming of him.

FINN WAS IN THE STUDY READING WHEN HE HEARD THE LARGE oaken door slam.

Nicolas was home.

"Where's Mercy?" Finn asked, seeing Nicolas was alone.

"At Amelia's, helping with something," Nicolas responded, in a distant way which suggested he had more important things on his mind than what Mercy was up to.

Finn wanted to ask how things went with the lawyers, but Nicolas' posture as he flopped down across from him forestalled the question.

He was slumped over in the chair, tie askance, dark hair pointing in several errant directions. Finn caught a whiff of the rank, potent alcohol on his breath. *Not good news, then.*

"You still love Ana," Nicolas stated with a weary sigh. It was not a question, simply a bridge to the point.

Finn nodded slowly.

"In order to make your son the heir, Ana needs to be married," Nicolas went on. He then stood back up in resignation, letting out an audible huff as he moved toward the wet bar, shakily pouring some Hennessy into a crystal glass. Finn imagined there'd been an internal battle raging prior to this moment, and Nicolas had lost.

Finn's breath caught in his chest as understanding slowly dawned. Nicolas was here to tell him Ana would be marrying Aidrik. He was about to say the one thing that might prevent Finn from going to her.

"I—" Finn started, but Nicolas put one hand up, as he took a long swallow of the amber liquid.

"The lawyers want you to marry her," Nicolas finished, setting the tumbler down. "Before the baby is born."

Finn's mouth opened, then closed. His heart felt as though it was dancing at the end of a rubber band as he processed the true meaning of Nic's frustrated exhaustion. "How? We don't even know where she is. And the baby will be here in less than a month…"

But, as Finn said these words, his mind was already formulating a plan.

"I don't know yet," Nicolas admitted, retaking his seat across from Finn. His eyes darted back toward the wet bar, and then dropped again. Finn knew about Nicolas' struggle with alcohol. He didn't know if Nicolas was an alcoholic, but he was aware the man often leaned on drink, rather than his own strength. He suspected Nicolas hated himself for it.

"Of course I'll marry her," Finn confirmed, resolutely holding his head higher than he had in months. "I wanted to before she left. Nothing has changed for me."

Nicolas looked up. His eyes were streaked with red. His face lined. "I'm not trying to wound you by saying this, but it's not you I'm worried about." For the first time Finn saw Nicolas struggling under the weight of family obligation, rather than the spirited playboy.

Finn nodded again, sympathetic understanding bringing an

encouraging smile to his face. "Ana will do it for our son. For his future."

"Do you really..." Nicolas trailed off, seeming to question whether he should say the words. Then, he forged ahead anyway. "Finn, do you really fucking want to marry someone who doesn't want you?"

Finn flinched but he understood Nicolas was trying to be kind.

He couldn't explain it. Nicolas hadn't been in his head down at the river, as he puzzled out his needs, separating them from his wants. Nicolas didn't know what he knew. He hadn't seen the look in Ana's eyes as she, reluctantly, walked away.

"Let that be my problem to solve," Finn decided. "Tell me what needs to happen."

3- TRISTAN

Tristan had been waiting his whole life to join the Deschanel Magi Collective. His mother, Elizabeth, first started mentioning it to him when he was barely out of diapers, whispering about the secretive club like it was The Knights Templar. She'd tell him stories, then stop in the middle and say, *Oh! The rest is secret... Collective ears only.* There was no intentional cruelty in her teasing, though it sadly had the effect of ostracizing him from the woman who'd birthed him, but could hardly be credited with raising him.

He knew enough, of course. The Collective had been around for centuries, and was created with the intention of cataloguing and understanding all the abilities Deschanels had manifested over the years. There was other business, but of course he was not privy to those endeavors. *When you turn twenty-one, you can decide if you want to be a member,* his mother explained. *That is, if they will have you.*

Yet, here Tristan was, several months shy of his twenty-first birthday, swearing the Fidelity Vow before his relatives. Aunt Colleen, the current magistrate, laid the crimson sash over his shoulder, and bade him repeat the oath:

In knowledge, comes power. In power, obligation. In obligation, commitment. In commitment, solidarity. In solidarity, enlightenment.

Tristan didn't know where the words came from, or even what the hell they meant. He only knew his heart was beating so hard he could hear it thumping in his ears like a low, heavy bass line. His sweaty palms nearly dropped the wine Aunt Evangeline passed his way. He had to resist the urge to knock it back, reminding himself he was in the presence of his elders and relatives, not his Catholic school buddies. *Sip, not chug.*

Tristan knew better than to question why he was allowed into the fold early. He only needed to look at the solemn, drawn faces of his aunts, uncles, and cousins. Something had happened. Something *bad*. Perhaps his strong telepathy was needed. There wasn't another living Deschanel whose mind-reading rivaled his, and he was the only one, to his knowledge, whose telepathy wasn't limited by distance.

He tried to pull an explanation from their minds, but he quickly realized it was no use. The Deschanels all knew how to block.

While everyone assembled, Tristan had taken mental attendance. There were two types of Deschanels in the room: members and council. There were far more members than council, as the latter group consisted of those in charge of setting the rules, deciding what members should and shouldn't know. The current council was only six, though a seventh would be chosen soon: Aunt Colleen, the magistrate, Aunt Evangeline, his mother Elizabeth, and then three cousins Tristan knew only in passing. Jasper Broussard, Pansy Guidry, and Luther Fontenot. The six were clearly marked by the shimmering flash of gold which ran down the center of their crimson sashes, otherwise identical to the ones everyone else in the room wore.

They already know why we're here. Tristan glanced between the six, looking for any expression that might betray their confidence, or give him even a hint of what was to come. All were stoic and unreadable, though. Even Jasper, who was well known in New Orleans for his theatrics, was oddly disquieted.

Tristan didn't need to wait long for his answers. As Colleen gathered the Collective around the massive mahogany table, she wasted no time in delivering explanations.

"The Council has recently learned the Deschanels are descended from a race of beings called Empyreans. It is this connection, in fact, that gives us our myriad of abilities," she began. Tristan first flinched, then felt his stomach drop to the floor. He looked around to see others' reactions but the faces were consistently passive and attentive.

There are at least three dozen members in this room. Not one of them is shocked by this revelation?

Glancing around at cousins, both familiar and unfamiliar, Tristan realized why their expressions remained neutral. Colleen often dropped knowledge bombs, in her matter-of-fact way, and so had conditioned the members against confusion and mayhem. This wasn't a debate, or a discussion intended to dissect the matter. The truth had been established, and she was simply catching everyone up so the playing field could be made equal.

Holyyyyy shit, she's serious, Tristan decided. *She told a room full of people we aren't entirely human, and not a single one freaked.*

Tristan listened in silence. Having taken cues from the other members on how to act, his inauguration was complete. Colleen could have declared the sun was going supernova in short order, and he wouldn't have uttered a peep. His heart raced in his excitement at being included, at being able to sit, side-by-side, with his mother as a peer. Finally.

"The Empyreans trace their roots to the origins of man, but at some point a mutation occurred, activating DNA dormant in humans. This DNA gave them their stronger abilities, longer lives, and a number of other peculiarities we don't yet fully understand."

A ripple of murmurs sounded, but no questions were asked.

"Many years ago, in the sixteenth century," Colleen went on, "an Empyrean, Aidrik, mated with one of our ancestors. This event imbued our family with Empyrean blood. Thus, we inherited diluted versions of their abilities."

Aidrik. Tristan knew that name somewhere. Hadn't he heard his mother whispering it, on the phone?

"But," Colleen said, her voice dropping lower, "as we have learned more about Aidrik and our ancestors, we have also learned about the Empyreans. In fact, we are about to welcome an Empyrean newborn into this family."

Here? In the family? Tristan's jaw nearly dropped, though a quick glance around the room showed neutral faces from his peers. Apparently he was the only one in the room surprised to learn they had descended from a *supernatural race of awesome beings.* A part of him wondered if this was an elaborate joke. Perhaps some bizarre hazing ritual for his initiation.

Tristan immediately knew better. He wouldn't put it past some of the wayward cousins in the room, but Colleen would *never* joke about such things.

One cousin on the Guidry side, Rene, opened his mouth to speak. Before he could form words, his mother, Pansy Guidry, raised one hand, laying it quickly, and decisively, across his cheek with a stinging slap. Whimpering, Rene quickly clapped his mouth shut, and Pansy's hand lowered again, without a word. Tristan recalled the Guidrys were often not welcome at family events, though no one had ever told him why. *Pansy is kind of a badass,* he concluded.

Colleen continued. "We know they are governed by a group called the Eldre Senetat, and we also know this group's intentions are not benevolent. They control the Empyreans through various manipulations, and set constricting rules to live by with penalty of death for breaking them. One of these rules is they are stringently prohibited from copulating with humans."

As Colleen paused to take a sip of her water, Tristan's aunt Evangeline spoke up. Although there was no formal Council hierarchy beyond the magistrate, Tristan always thought of Evangeline as the second-in-command, based on his mother's scattered insights. "The Senetat is unaware of the Deschanels' existence because of a protection Aidrik put over the family, and *Ophélie*, many years ago. But a new situation has come up which makes us all vulnerable. The family is now at risk."

"Yes, that is why we are here tonight," Colleen cut in, resuming command. "Anasofiya attempted to take her own life a few months ago." At this, Tristan finally observed the collective shocks and gasps he had been waiting for. He marveled this bit of information, and not the revelation they were some sort of quasi-superheroes, is what would invoke it.

Redirecting the emotion in the room, Aunt Colleen expanded, "Aidrik, our ancestor, was there. He saved her life. In doing so, he fused a part of his DNA to hers, employing a rare process called Sveising. This *changed* Ana, making her more Empyrean than human. It also changed her unborn child, who will be born into this world not human, but Empyrean."

This brought shared looks from members around the table. The Council simply nodded, clearly already aware of the disclosures being made today.

"Ana is pregnant?" Anne, one of Tristan's cousins, wondered aloud. Her pale hair bobbed in its ponytail, as her head whipped around. "Is it... Finn's?"

Tristan had to stifle a giggle. Anne had a crush on Finn ever since she first met him. Tristan's mother gossiped about it all the time. *She's wasting her time. The boy only has eyes for Ana.*

"Yes, and yes," Colleen replied, curtly. Anne looked stricken. This was a double blow. Not only was Finn even further from her reach than she initially thought, but her beloved mentor, Colleen, had kept something from her.

"And, as I said, the Sveising changed the unborn child, but mutating the genes to be more Empyrean than human was only part of the transformation. Now, this child is not simply Ana and Finn's, but also Aidrik's."

"We discussed this, Colleen. You know this is impossible," Tristan's mother, Elizabeth, interjected. "A child cannot have more than one father. As a doctor, you shouldn't continue to repeat such silly things."

"Yes, we *did* discuss this already," Colleen chided, clearly displeased a fellow Council member would disagree in this forum, even if that Council member was her sister. "An Empyrean child can. And in fact, many do. Multiple fathers give Empyreans an advantage a child with only one father does not have. Greater strengths."

Elizabeth shook her head in disbelief, but said no more.

"Go on, Colleen," Councilman Luther Fontenot urged. "We don't have to like it to be in accord."

She flashed him a small, grateful smile, and went on. "The challenge facing us is this: it is unlikely this birth will escape the Senetat's notice. If Ana, Aidrik, and the child are discovered, their lives will be in mortal danger. But beyond that, it will launch a chain reaction of events which will potentially expose this entire family to the Senetat." Colleen shifted her eyes between each person in the room before dropping her final bombshell. "Every single one of us is a violation of their laws. They would annihilate us."

Tristan couldn't help himself anymore. He was bursting with questions. "But, based on their laws, isn't the only criminal this Aidrik dude? And whoever he banged back in the day?"

A few snickers rippled across the room. Tristan's mother tensed up, defensively.

"If these were the laws of our people, I would say you were

correct," Colleen responded, gently. Her words subtly admonished those who had ridiculed Tristan for his question. She was showing him it was safe and Tristan fought back the inappropriate smile which wanted to bloom in appreciation of her kindness. "But the Senetat operates by their own rules. We are a threat to them."

"How so?" Tristan pressed, with newfound confidence. "We can't even be half as powerful as they are!"

No titters this time. "We're a threat to their authority," Colleen clarified, smiling at her nephew. "If other Empyreans learned of our existence, and knew the Senetat did nothing about it, it would undermine their influence. They would have no choice but to destroy us."

Tristan thought he understood. He'd read enough high fantasy to know there were laws and then there were *laws.* If no being existed who was powerful enough to hold the Senetat accountable, or put into doubt their potency, then they'd continue to do as they pleased.

"What you're saying makes it seem like there's no hope," Remy Fontenot, Luther's son, said. "Are you suggesting we wait for them to come murder us?"

"Not at all," Colleen replied, her calm demeanor never showing even a single crack. "Aidrik has a plan to engage a subset of the Empyrean population, rebels known as Runeans. They have long been adversaries of the Senetat, living in secret, waiting for a reason to strike. Their cohesiveness has lacked a strong leader to unite them. Aidrik believes he knows the right person to lead this revolution. They are planning to recruit him, in hopes they can attempt a maneuver before the Senetat discovers the deception. However, first, Ana must deliver a healthy son, and heir."

More questions were fired across the table. They wanted to know more about the Runeans, about this supposed leader Aidrik was planning to engage, and what their planned coup maneuver entailed. Some wanted to join the fight. Others, now understanding the true scope of the specialized safe haven, wanted to help with Nicolas and Mercy's efforts at *Ophélie*.

Tristan absorbed everything, like an eager disciple.

Markus, Evangeline's son, wanted to know if they had a live, or dead, Empyrean they could dissect and study.

Antoine Guidry, another of Pansy's vast brood, inquired about whether or not the family had a proper fallout bunker. Just in case.

Leander Broussard, Jasper's son, wasn't clear why they hadn't simply written Ana and her son off as collateral damage, in order to protect the family.

Amelia Jameson, Colleen's daughter, was aghast anyone was even *thinking* about abandoning another Deschanel.

As each of Tristan's cousins took their turns expressing a viewpoint, his mind began to wander, marveling at how the entire family's world changed in a matter of minutes. It then made him wonder what other secrets he had yet to learn about the family... and how much *other* crazy shit went down at a gathering of the Deschanel Magi Collective.

"I'll go," Anne announced, standing proudly. Tristan blinked, realizing he had missed a whole piece of the conversation.

"You don't even *like* your cousin," Elizabeth scoffed. Tristan blushed. His mother sounded like a teenage girl.

Fire burned behind Anne's eyes, and Tristan worried for a moment one of the bushes outside might burst through the window and strangle his mother. Anne was, after all, an arborkinetic. And it wouldn't be the first time she'd killed someone with her "gift."

"That is not true," Anne asserted, the blaze subsiding as Colleen laid a soothing hand against the girl's waist. "I don't like what she's done to Finn, that's all."

"You would be a good choice, my dear," Colleen said, gently guiding Anne back down to her chair. "Your talent with flora could come in handy. We know Ana and Aidrik are somewhere in the wilds of Wales. Your experience as a midwife in the bayou may prove useful as well, if Ana goes into labor. Thank you for volunteering, but you can't go alone." Her last statement resulted in another pointed look around the table.

Wales. Ana and Aidrik. This was a rescue mission! Tristan flew from his seat. "Send me!"

Elizabeth started so hard at this she nearly toppled out of her chair. "My child is *not* going to traipse around the United Kingdom with some crazy, immortal cult leaders on his trail! Absolutely not, nope, not even considering it!"

"Elizabeth, get ahold of yourself," Luther admonished, sighing under his breath.

Tristan was often embarrassed by his mother's outbursts, but at least this time he wasn't tethered by them. "I'm not a child anymore. I'm old enough to decide for myself, and I want to go."

"Tristan would be a good choice," Evangeline concurred, nodding her head thoughtfully. "He's a powerful telepath. We'll need a way to communicate with whoever goes. He could keep us abreast of things, as well as keeping our dear Anne safe."

Anne blushed at this, and Tristan saw one of her tiny fists clench. She apparently did not take well to it being implied she was helpless.

"Oh, how you Deschanels like to coddle your youth!" Pansy declared. "Why, you'll turn this boy into a crying little girl if no one stops you! Is he gonna borrow your dresses, too?"

"He's my *only* child now!" Elizabeth cried. She buried her face in her hands and began to sob, in her usual melodramatic fashion. "He's all I have…"

Tristan didn't need to be reminded about his sister's death. Nor did he need his mother capitalizing on it for attention. "I'm going. It's settled."

It wasn't settled. At least, not right away. The debate raged for another hour, Elizabeth demanding her son be disqualified, others insisting it was a wise choice. Tristan declaring it was *his* choice, wise or not.

But his mother eventually grew weary, as she often did when emotions were involved. Evangeline escorted her home as the rest of the group dissembled, taking overlong with their pleasantries and goodbyes. Tristan patiently remained behind, to thank Colleen for believing in him, and allowing him to be a part of this important mission for their family.

All at once, it occurred to him why he'd been brought into the Collective early. *Aunt C planned this all along. She knew I would volunteer. She knew I needed to get away from here. From my mother.*

Tristan understood, with a sudden rush of mature-feeling insight, it was in little ways, such as this, that Aunt Colleen had been more of a mother to him than Elizabeth had ever been. He was not nearly as abandoned as he sometimes felt.

"You have a good heart, Tristan," Colleen said. Anne and Tristan helped her as she put away the candles and china. "But don't mistake this for an adventure. I don't know what the three of you will find."

"Three?" Tristan realized he had missed more of the conversation than he initially thought.

"You, Anne, and Finn," Colleen replied, with a hint of chastisement in her voice. She knew he hadn't been paying full attention.

"Finn is going to marry Ana," Anne explained, with a troubled twist of her lips. "We're his escorts."

Interesting. Well, it still beat the hell out of laying in bed playing video games.

4- ANNE

Anne regretted slamming her bedroom door, but it didn't mean the sentiment wasn't sincere.

Downstairs, Colleen would be upset. Upset Anne was hurting, but more so, that Anne either could not, or would not, control her distress. Anne was still learning to govern her moods, because the unrestrained temper of an emotional arborkinetic never led to anything good.

Don't pack more than you can easily carry in a camper's backpack, Aunt Colleen had said.

I'll start thinking about what I should take tomorrow...

No, dear. Tonight. You must leave in the morning.

The morning!

Time is of the essence. We don't know how long it will take you to find Ana. There's nothing more to plan.

Then, Colleen placed a calming hand against Anne's cheek. It was soothing, despite her agitation. Colleen had all but adopted her several years prior, taking Anne under her wing and giving her not only a home, but a loving mentor and friend. Colleen was the last person in the world Anne wanted to let down.

All at once, the nervous anxiety fluttered up inside of her. *Tomorrow*. But, that was so soon! She'd barely learned she would be going. She needed time to process this. Time to let her mind come around to the idea.

It had taken Anne years before she ventured out of the bayou, and into New Orleans, to find her family. She'd been born a bastard of Charles Deschanel, Colleen's brother, a secret kept from Anne most of her life. It was only upon her mother's death she felt brave enough to journey to the city and find her sister, Adrienne, and brother, Nicolas.

But while her half-siblings had embraced her, Colleen had done so much more. Taught her how to summon plant life freely, and not as an unintentional reaction to her moods. Had even showed her how to commune with them. It wasn't anything like talking to people. Anne couldn't have described it with mere words. But she understood the plants, and they understood her. Colleen's expansive Uptown estate, aptly named The Gardens, was the perfect place to practice these newfound skills.

And now, she would be venturing away from her home, and her foundation. Her truest supporter. Joining her would be a smartass cousin she hardly knew, and a man she thought she could love, if he would only see her.

But Finn didn't see her. He never would. His heart would ever and always belong to the undeserving Ana. And he was willfully blind to the reality she didn't reciprocate his feelings.

Anne scolded herself for disliking her cousin. Aunt Elizabeth had accused her of not liking Ana, and Anne had lied when she denied the allegation. How could she like a woman who hurt a man as good, and true, as Finnegan St. Andrews?

No, Anne wasn't going out of any love for her cousin, Ana. And she wasn't really going because of Finn, at least not entirely. She was going because she had never, in the years she had lived with her, ever seen Colleen look so desperate. So helpless. Anne thought it was seeing their venerable, strong leader in such a state that kept the group's reactions at bay. Colleen could have revealed her intentions to murder them all, and they'd have watched her, quietly and reverently, as they had tonight. They respected and loved her that much.

Anne respected and loved her that much, too. She would put aside her fears of the unknown, her envy at Finn's misplaced devotion, and trek bravely forth.

COLLEEN'S DRIVER DROPPED ANNE OFF SLIGHTLY AFTER FIVE IN the morning. The spring air was unusually chilly, and her nervous breath clouded miserably before her face.

Tristan was already there. He stood huddled with Nicolas, Mercy, and Finn on the expansive lower gallery of *Ophélie*. Anne wondered why they weren't inside, keeping warm, but Colleen's words from the night before came to her. *Time is of the essence.*

Anne took a moment to study her travel mates. Tristan wore the excited face of a young hobbit going on his first adventure. Finn's expression was harder to read. He was deep in thought, reflecting. If she tried hard enough, she could use her limited telepathy to read his mind. But likely the Deschanels had taught him to block.

"I appreciate what you two are doing," Finn stated, finally, breaking the silence.

"We're family," Tristan answered. "You're one of us now." Some of the excitement had dissolved from his countenance. He seemed to be attempting a transition into a more serious frame of mind.

"Yes, family," Anne repeated, thinking again of how the Deschanels had embraced her when she'd been alien to them. "We'll do our best to help you."

"That little fucker growing in Ana's belly is my heir, so I sure as shit *hope* you'll do your best!" Nicolas exclaimed. He had an arm draped around Mercy, who said nothing.

The rest of the small talk was unmemorable to Anne. All that remained of the exchange was the final moment, just before they left to catch their private flight from the nearby airfield.

Finn embraced Nicolas in what was either the most awkward, or most endearing, hug in the history of the world. Even stranger, Nicolas returned it, whispering in Finn's ear, *You* are *family now, brother. Come back to us safely.*

5- AIDRIK

Aidrik remained alert long after the fire died to glowing coals. He did not expect to sleep much this eve. Rest had become irrelevant as Anasofiya's condition worsened.

It would be preferable to take her somewhere with acceptable accommodations. Somewhere with warm water, and sturdy walls against the inclement weather. There was a limit to what comfort he could create, in this tumbledown manor, with vines older than her peeking through cracks in the brick, and the sky half-visible through what remained of the ceiling.

But he could not risk detection. Her life was in peril here, but would be entirely forfeit if they were discovered by the Senetat.

As a mystic, he had been blessed with many different abilities, whereas most were lucky to have one. Among other things, he was a shaman, and a telepath, but also a seer. Of his abilities, this one was the least potent, and thus, the most dangerous. His visions were incomplete, and unpredictable. He saw Anasofiya lying in her own blood. He saw her thriving. He did not know which reality would come to culmination. Ambiguity drove him mad. Fear besieged him. It was a unique experience for him to have something to lose that he could not live without.

Aidrik kept vigilant watch as her sleeping figure drew weary, ragged breaths. Carrying a child to term was traumatic for an Empyrean of full blood, so it was of little wonder the havoc it wrought on Anasofiya, who was still partly of Man. Though Aidrik laid his healing hands on her, night after night, day after day, she grew steadily weaker. Slept more. Ate less. Cried out in her fitful sleep.

Aidrik knew Anasofiya's tears were from a pain far deeper than anything physical she was experiencing. She was strong; very strong. Never complained once about the physical toll their son was taking on her, instead choosing to embrace the beauty, and promise, in the life she carried. All the while, this other thing, this malady Aidrik could not fix, consumed her.

Men would call what afflicted her *melancholia.* It was a notion Aidrik, and most Empyreans, were entirely unfamiliar with. Aside from the evigbond—that sacred, irreversible connection between two individuals of Empyrean bloodlines—Empyreans did not form attachments. They were a race of beings who lived thousands of years. Mourning and sentiment were impractical and unreasonable.

Anasofiya was in mourning. She made a valiant attempt to hide it from him, but he had not survived four millennia by being unobservant. He saw her turn her head when tears flowed, and noticed the frequency with which she was lost to her thoughts. He heard her call out Finn's name in her agitated sleep.

It mystified him. Anasofiya was his evigbond. This was indisputable. It was not a choice, but a chemical fusion, connecting them forever. And choice or no, Aidrik loved her deeply.

Anasofiya had appeared confident in her choice when they left Louisiana. Her tears at leaving Finn were a reasonable reaction in a Child of Man. They had been in a relationship. She had conceived by him.

In the first few months away, she seemed happy, and content. Resolved.

Then, the stretches of quiet began. She stopped sharing her thoughts openly. Started spending more time alone.

What most complicated this for Aidrik the Wise was he knew Anasofiya loved him even more than the day she left with him. If she no longer wanted him, the choice would be simple. His heart and soul would be rent asunder, but he would release her. What tore his *Kjære* apart was her dawning realization she could not live without both halves of her heart.

It was apparent now that Aidrik only held one-half.

ANASOFIYA AWOKE JUST AFTER DAWN. AIDRIK HAD unintentionally drifted into a light rest, and the sound startled him. In one swift motion, Ulfberht was drawn, and Anasofiya gasped, falling back against the stone wall. Aidrik's robe, which she had been wrapped in all night, fell aside. As it did, her swollen, grotesque belly protruded from under her shabby sweatshirt.

"Aidrik, it's me."

"Apologies, *Kjære.* I did not realize my slumber." Aidrik sheathed Ulfberht, maddened at himself for such repose.

Anasofiya flashed him a forgiving smile, and as she did the bags under her eyes seemed large and bruising, making her face appear devoid of life. A cold chill pierced his heart.

"Allow me to heat sustenance for breaking your fast," Aidrik implored, with a heavy tenderness. He was not used to being so aware of each spoken word. But he feared one wrong remark could drive her further away.

She pulled the hooded mantle, wrapping it back around her.

Shifting uncomfortably, she lay down and closed her eyes. "I'm still so tired. Let me rest a little longer."

Aidrik leaned in and smoothed her hair off her forehead. His lips pressed against it.

"Elsker, Kjære," he whispered. I love you, dearest.

She offered a wan smile at this, and slipped one cold hand through this. "I know," she replied sleepily.

Within moments, Anasofiya's sleep continued restlessly, her stretched and tired body curled into a loose ball. Instinctively, he reached out to soothe her, allowing the transfer of healing energies to pass from him, to her. She calmed, settling back into a more relaxed slumber. For now. But Aidrik remained troubled.

He was losing her. Physically, and emotionally. He believed he could fix the first, but he knew of no solution for the second.

6- FINN

Wales in the spring was startlingly cold. But Finn grew up in the northern Atlantic, and the Welsh air felt a bit like home. After a few months in humid Louisiana, he almost welcomed the crisp, chilled air filling his lungs.

Anne suffered in silence as they slogged through the spring snow outside Cardiff Airport. Conversely, Tristan made his discomfort known with every step, mumbling and cursing about adventures and video games. Finn ignored them both, signing for the tiny rental car.

While Anne and Tristan bickered over who was least competent to drive, claiming neither had ever mastered a manual transmission, Finn slid in behind the wheel and deftly started the efficient engine. Drawing from his natural navigational skills, within minutes, he'd adjusted to driving on the left side of the road, and they were off. Contrite and embarrassed, his companions said not another word.

Outside Swansea, Finn pulled over at a small pub, Môr Teg, for lunch. Entirely focused on finding Ana, he was not the least bit hungry, but Anne and Tristan needed to eat. They also needed time to gather their bearings. Maneuvering a foreign country, with limited direction, would take some coordination.

"So, we ready to get this party started?" Tristan proposed, face buried in his meat pie.

Anne looked up at Finn, and he met her gaze. She seemed to understand what Tristan in his youthful invincibility did not: this was dangerous. For every peril they knew about, there were numerous others lurking undefined.

"Perhaps you should readjust your expectations, Tristan," Anne responded, evenly.

Tristan ignored her, winking at Finn. Finn could see what the ever-serious Anne failed to, that Tristan was trying to insert some needed levity. His natural inclination was to use humor as a coping mechanism for stress. "So, I think we should drive around aimlessly until they jump out in front of the car and yell 'Surprise!'"

Anne sighed. Finn gazed down at his untouched stew. He'd left his appetite behind in Louisiana. Lacking solid information, their plan of attack was vague and hopeful, at best. Colleen and Nicolas had gone through pictures of abandoned castles together, looking for the one Nicolas saw in his visions of Ana. They'd managed to narrow it down to four possibilities, which Colleen marked for them on a map, four arrows drawn in a red gel pen. Finn was skeptical, but what else did they have? In the end, he'd search every corner of Wales if he had to.

"We will find them," Anne broke the silence. She gave Finn another meaningful look. He quickly dropped his eyes again.

Anne was a kindhearted girl. He enjoyed her company when she came to wander the gardens at *Ophélie,* and appreciated how she never forced him to talk about Ana, or all that had happened. Being around Nicolas and Mercy reminded him of the whole, terrible situation, but Anne was a reprieve from his tortured thoughts.

She was a friend, though Finn was all too aware she secretly hoped they could be more. In another life, or in different circumstances, Finn might have entertained it, but he was who he was. Once he'd given his heart to Anasofiya Deschanel, it was no longer his to barter. And if the situation in Wales didn't work out as he hoped, he would never give it away again.

"What if they aren't here anymore?" Tristan asked. He finished his pie, and was picking at the bread on Finn's plate. Anne shot him a censuring look he missed entirely, but Finn didn't mind. He wasn't going to eat it.

"They will be," Anne said confidently. "Ana is..." she trailed off, looking at Finn, "not well," she finished. "They're awaiting the arrival of her son."

Not well. Ana had been *not well* for many years, but this was different. Mercy had explained to Finn that Empyrean women only gave birth once, due to the traumatic toll it took on the mother's body. Ana was not fully Empyrean, yet was giving birth to an Empyrean child. Her body was understandably shutting down.

Aidrik can help her... right? Finn had asked Mercy. Aidrik was a powerful shaman. He'd brought Ana back from the precipice of death once before. And Finn now knew Ana was a healer as well.

But Mercy had merely shrugged. She'd spent three thousand years as an Empyrean, only to die and be resurrected a mortal human. There were no guarantees in life. She wouldn't fill Finn's head with false promises. And though his heart sank at the uncertainty, he appreciated her honesty. He would rather know the rough path ahead than walk down it blindly.

Anne pulled out a large map, and pressed it against the pub window. The light from outside shone through, illuminating it. "The first castle is in Pencoed, which is about a half-hour drive from here. We'll start with that one. From there, we will take a short drive to nearby Ruperra, for the second. The third is in Tegfynydd, which will take us another hour or so. By the way, I have no idea if I'm saying any of these names right." She traced her finger up the western coastline, stopping just before the Irish Sea. "The last one is at the far north end of Wales. Gwyn-fryn. About a half-day's drive, depending on the weather. I figure we can search the first three by evening, provided the properties are small enough, and then start for the last one, if necessary, in the morning. Ideally, even if Ana is distracted by her condition, Aidrik will sense our presence and make theirs known."

Finn allowed himself an inward sigh of relief. He was grateful Anne assumed command and provided a plan. His mind was too busy formulating how to convince Ana she should accept the proposal he planned to make. Not even Tristan and Anne knew. He didn't want to deal with either of them trying to talk him out of it, which they undoubtedly would.

He was equally glad they would spend only days, not weeks, searching. Wales was not an especially large country, but in his mind he'd pictured them wandering aimlessly across the moors, poking their head into one abandoned building after another.

If Anne was correct, they would find Ana and Aidrik before sunset tomorrow.

7- NICOLAS

"You need to keep trying," Colleen was saying through the phone. "I'll send Amelia over later. Sometimes the presence of an empath—"

"You're not listening, Aunt C," Nicolas protested wearily. "I can't summon these visions. Ana either sends them, or she doesn't. It ain't video-on-demand."

"Yes, I know that has been the course thus far," Colleen replied, with a hint of testiness, "but we still have no idea as to the scope of your mystic abilities. It's entirely possible you can initiate this connection on your own. We won't know if you don't try. And you can't try if you're busy sulking around that enormous plantation of yours."

"I don't sulk," Nicolas disputed, sulking. "And these visions are useless. What good is trying to interpret what a seer sees if he can't even make up his mind whether it's raining or sunny?"

Aunt Colleen made an exasperated sound that reminded him of how she used to chastise him as a child. "Even if they are unreliable, they're more than what we have without them. They present to us, at the very least, potential outcomes we can analyze. And plan for. I don't think I need to remind you how important planning is at this stage."

"No—"

"Do pull it together. For Ana."

Nicolas widened his eyes in shock at the dial tone resonating in his ear. "Holy shit. She hung up on me."

"Try not to look so surprised," Mercy muttered, from across the study. She was reading through some of the documentation Sullivan & Associates sent over for the project they were getting ready for, sheltering the children of Empyrean Runean rebels. There would be a battle, after Ana delivered her son, after she and Aidrik engaged the rebels in their common cause. Once the Runeans rose up against the Senetat, nothing would remain certain. *Ophélie* was safe, and protected, so Nicolas had offered to house the Runean offspring, allowing the parents to focus on what lay ahead. "You really are being ridiculous," she added.

Mercy's silver hair fell like shards of ice on the pages as she leaned over the paperwork. Her reading glasses sat perched on the end of her nose, though Nicolas was a bit surprised she hadn't thrown them across the room yet. Even the need for them was an offense to Mercy, who had gone from being three thousand years old and immortal, to a very normal human woman in her twenties. Declining vision, and all.

"Oh? How's that?" Nicolas challenged.

Mercy slid the glasses off, and looked up. "Do you have any inkling the amount of wasted effort that goes into sulking? I've never known of anyone who saved the day by walking around with a magnificent scowl on their face. Have you?"

Nicolas had a few stinging retorts loaded and ready, but, for once, his heart wasn't in it. "If you have a better idea, Clementyn, perhaps now's the time to share it."

"Your aunt already did. Focus. Spend some actual time trying to figure out who you are, and what you can do."

"I have," he protested, but it was a weak defense. Her raised eyebrow indicated she knew it, too.

"Nicolas," she put her paperwork aside and crossed the room toward him, "you've never had to put effort into anything in your life. Why, look at these beautiful, callous-free hands," Mercy teased, flipping his palms over with a slow shake of her head. "But for the rest of the world, effort usually involves exerting some real energy toward goals."

Nicolas narrowed his eyes as he snatched his hands back. "Your world view isn't exactly fucking normal, either," he accused. "If I say I can't do it, then I can't."

Mercy's face softened. "I know you're worried for Ana."

"You don't know a damn thing about it!" Nicolas snapped, then put a hand up in surrender. "Yes, I'm anxious. But trying to get into Aidrik's fucking head isn't going to make me less concerned. Do you have any idea what crazy shit I see in his visions?"

"But it might help Anne, Tristan, and Finn," Mercy suggested. "Especially if anything has changed since your last nested vision. This isn't a situation we want them walking into blindly."

He released a frustrated, and rather loud, sigh. Colleen said essentially the same thing at the start of their conversation. But that wasn't what was bothering him. "I should have gone with them," he asserted, putting voice to it. "Why the hell didn't I?"

"You know why," Mercy replied, with a pointed glance, gesturing toward the stacks of paperwork on the desk behind her. "None of this can happen without you."

By "this" she meant their crazy idea that they could somehow help change the course of history. They hadn't used those words, not exactly, but it was certainly their intention when they agreed to harbor the offspring of the Runean rebels. *I can never have children, but I can still be a mother in other ways,*

Mercy had said. Not much tugged at the heartstrings of Nicolas Deschanel, but that had done it.

He was not persuaded purely by her maternal longings. After nearly thirty-one years, and all that had happened in the last of them, something about this mission called to him. For the first time, he had a semblance of an idea about who he was, where he'd come from, and redeeming purpose in a previously self-indulgent life. He'd been afflicted by an innate urge to protect all of these learnings, in any way he could. Giving the Runean leaders some comfort before they stood up against the Eldre Senetat was the course they'd chosen.

Ophélie was under strong protection from Aidrik. The children would be safe.

But, there was a lot of work to be done.

"I hate this," Nicolas moaned, flopping back in a chair, defeated.

Mercy had the good sense not to twist his words into a personal affront. "Ana is well-protected. She could not be safer than she is with Aidrik. And Finn is on his way to her." She knelt before him, looking up into his troubled eyes. "Perhaps you're having trouble letting go of being her protector?"

Something had grown between Nicolas and Mercy, something he still struggled to define, and wasn't sure yet he even wanted to, but this was one topic he couldn't discuss with her. "I will *always* protect, Ana. No matter who else loves her, or looks over her, or knocks her up. And that is something not even you, in your infinite wisdom, could ever understand. If you can't accept it? Leave."

He stood up in a rush of stubbornness and untenable frustration, leaving Mercy to whatever interpretation she wished.

WHEN SHE DIDN'T JOIN HIM AT BEDTIME, NICOLAS KNEW HE'D

gone too far. Even solid, patient Mercy had her limits. He was ashamed for feeling it was okay to test them.

He knew instinctively going after her would be futile. He'd crossed a line, and she would let him know when he was allowed back over it.

As he drifted off to sleep, he felt the invisible hands close around his mind, pulling him away from his immediate reality. It was not a nested vision; he initiated those. This was a skill he hadn't yet learned to summon on his own, and wasn't even sure he actually possessed. *Dream fuckery,* he called it, though he was sure there was a less colorful, more official term for it. Colleen seemed to think he could do it wide-awake, if he focused enough, but Nicolas wasn't sure he wanted to.

Getting into the mind of Ana had been one thing. He knew her brain like his own. But Aidrik's psyche was a vast canyon of unknown horrors. Behind one rock, he might see a vision of death and destruction. Another might reveal an intimate moment he had no business seeing. And yet another might be so utterly mundane it would threaten to put him to sleep if he wasn't already.

But all of it, every moment, with Aidrik, was a vision of the future. Not always what would be, but definitely what could. The difficulty was the impossibility in discerning the difference.

This time, it was Aidrik again, as if Colleen's requests were seeping into Nicolas' subconscious to help him deliver. Similar to the other visions, there were no words, only a flash of images. But this sequence was more concentrated, more powerful, than any of the others. Each rock he turned over revealed something more disturbing than the last. Ana, standing on a stone precipice, looking over the edge. Light glinting off Aidrik's sword, as it slashed through the air. Ana, lying in a pool of blood, unmoving. Aidrik, standing before a jury of men in red robes. Ana raising her hands to the sky in unparalleled rage.

As the images intensified, Nicolas' heart rate skyrocketed,

and his breath came so rapidly he worried there wasn't enough air in the room to sustain him. He threw his arms out, looking for something, anything, to grip on to and bring him out of this, but there was nothing.

Finally, two strong, but soft, hands shook him. His eyes flashed open, and Mercy sat astride him, her expression more solemn, and troubled, than he'd ever seen it.

"You're crying," she whispered in wonder, tenderly brushing her warm hands over his face as he continued to gasp for air, processing his escape from the vision. *Safe.*

"I'm sorry," he whispered through his tears, words which rarely ever escaped the mouth of Nicolas Deschanel. "I'm so sorry."

"I know," Mercy replied, and pressed her lips to his, enveloping him in the comfort he worried he didn't deserve, but desperately needed.

8- ANNE

Pencoed Castle was reportedly in utter ruin. Not that Anne expected anything less from an abandoned fortress, but she knew, sight unseen, Ana and Aidrik would not be there.

They trekked forth, despite her lack of confidence. They had to be sure, before moving on. *Time is of the essence,* Colleen had said. Every moment that went by put the family closer to ruin, though Anne knew finding Ana and Aidrik would not change that troubling fact. But Ana delivering her child, in wedlock, and returning to health, meant she and Aidrik could move forward with their plan to organize the Runeans toward the reality of a revolution.

When they passed through the village of Llanmartin to ask for directions, an old shopkeeper gave them a searching glance. *Pencoed? Why, no'one goes there n'more. The grass and birds ha' greater claim than its owner.*

Approaching the derelict property, Anne knew exactly what the old man meant. The large, stone gatehouse, three stories high, flanked by square turrets was covered in vines snaking from the base all the way to the top of crumbling towers. The ashlar stone looked like it grew right out of the untouched snowdrifts, the white magnifying years of wear and tear. The buildings behind were masked almost entirely by foliage, with only glimpses of stone peeking through the cover.

Well, I can do something about that, at least.

"They're not here," Tristan said, massaging himself for warmth. He looked as if he'd been dropped in a bucket of ice. His chestnut hair, peeking out of the jacket he'd zipped up over half his face, looked as if it hadn't been combed in weeks, sticking out in thirteen different directions. Strangely, she had the impression he styled it that way *intentionally*. Equally idiotic was the sporadic patches of hair on his face which were clearly intended to make him appear older. The effect was lost on Anne, who thought the result only made him look like a lanky man-baby. "I am not sensing anything."

"No, you wouldn't," Anne replied. "Aidrik is an Empyrean. Ana is... well, no one knows anymore. But she's a Deschanel, and so she's obviously capable of blocking us." She said the last as if to imply, *use your damn head.* But Anne would have never said anything so cruel aloud, no matter her level of pique.

Tristan looked properly ashamed at Anne's reminder, and said no more.

"But," Anne continued, "I don't think they're here, either. We still have to do our due diligence, though. It wouldn't do well at all if we went all the way to north Wales, only to have to double back because we didn't properly search."

Tristan nodded, but Finn said nothing, moving swiftly toward the gatehouse. Anne was almost glad she couldn't read his thoughts. She knew they would be filled with *Ana, Ana, Ana...*

"Wait," she called, halting Finn. "Let me."

Finn stepped to the side. His eyes grew wide as he realized what she was planning. But he'd seen it before. Their very first introduction had been by way of her special abilities.

Anne closed her eyes, and focused on bringing forth the energies from deep, deep within her. The snow around her feet started to gust and swirl, then melt, as heat radiated outward from her tiny frame. The whole farmyard surrounding the castle seemed to tremor, and then a low, guttural screeching arose from the stone monolith as the vines began to peel themselves back, exposing the buildings. As the foliage receded, a few chickens scrambled for new cover amid squawks of indignant protest.

"Never gets old," Finn remarked with a short breath.

"Badass," Tristan added.

As Anne lowered her arms, the sounds dimmed and the wind receded. It was getting easier now. She could do it without utterly exhausting herself.

But it did still embarrass her, for others to see her talents. She blushed, and then hurried ahead so the two men wouldn't see it.

The sky was cloudy and dark above them, the sun hidden behind dense fog. As they stepped through the opening of the gatehouse, Anne had the distinct, awful feeling of walking into death and decay. If Ana and Aidrik *were* here, nothing good had become of them.

Stepping into a dilapidated courtyard, they came upon what had been a great Tudor mansion. The windows were all busted out, with the frames hanging haphazardly in some openings. Great numbers of rooks and pigeons ruffled and cooed. As the aged shopkeeper had claimed, birds were the only inhabitants Pencoed had housed in many years.

The interior was even worse. The great hall, likely once a place of merriment and celebration, was filled with debris and bird droppings, snowdrifts piled inside the window frames. A crumbling hearth was framed by more rogue vines also splattered thickly with bird scat. Her nose detected a strong ammonia scent, an indication perhaps larger animals had taken shelter here also.

Anne heard crunching, and turned to see Finn off ahead, on his own. Tufts of his sandy blonde hair peeked out from under his wool hat and she thought, as she often did, about how nice it would be to touch him. To run her hands through the soft curls, and see him smile, really smile. To trace her finger over the tiny scar on his lip... or the other one, across his chest, that she glimpsed by accident when she came upon him stripping off his clothes after a day on the river. The jagged white line bisected his torso, cutting through the curve of his taught muscles. Something about seeing this resilient man was actually not infallible made her stomach swim with desire. It hurt her to even look at Finn. If only she could steal even one moment alone with him...

She moved to follow him, but Tristan looked at her and shook his head, quickly. Finn wanted, or needed, to be alone.

Anne bit back her frustration. It was irrational for her to begrudge him the desires of his heart. But nothing felt rational standing in this abandoned, neglected mansion, miles and miles from home.

So, they spread out. Anne took the west wing, Finn the east, and Tristan scoured the outside grounds. An hour later they wandered back toward the gatehouse, all reporting what each of them, instinctively, already knew: Ana and Aidrik were not there. Nor was there any sign of recent human presence, like a fire or campsite.

"At least we can scratch one off the list!" Tristan said cheerily, making a tick swipe in the air with his finger. "That makes us twenty-five percent closer to our goal... at worst."

This was obviously an effort to lighten the somber mood. But Tristan's glass-half-full outlook on the situation wasn't contagious. Finn walked back to the car in silence, and Anne followed, helpless.

9- TRISTAN

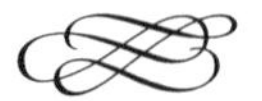

Pencoed had been a bust. Nearby Ruperra Castle produced equal results. Tegfynydd was an hour away, and would be their last stop for the evening. If that visit didn't bear fruit, they'd head for their last destination, Gwyn-fryn, in the morning. Tristan felt heartened each stop brought them closer to their goal, though Finn and Anne only grew quieter with each dead end.

Of course, there was always the possibility *none* of these castles were the right one. Nicolas' visions were sketchy at best. There had to be hundreds of castles in Wales! What would they do if they had to start from scratch?

Tension mounted despite no one voicing these doubts, and Tristan was growing weary of trying to keep the mood upbeat. He was jet-lagged, cold, and the gravity of what was on their shoulders had finally set in.

There were so many things that could go wrong. Having grown up the son of Elizabeth Sullivan, the consummate worrier, Tristan was predisposed to cataloguing his doubts and dwelling on them. If they didn't find Ana, Nicolas would have to choose another heir. If they did find Ana, and she turned Finn away, the same result. And if they were somehow detected by this Senetat, it was all over.

Tristan tried not to think too much about the results. The promise of being useful, and escaping his domineering mother, were not his only reasons for volunteering to come. Though Tristan had never been close to Ana—who really was, except Nicolas?—she'd always been kind to him. And in her own way, she tried to show him comfort during those intervals when she recognized his upbringing was especially challenging.

He recalled how, when she learned he was being bullied in school, she'd pop her arm out of its socket and then heal herself, over and over, to make him laugh. It worked, too. He could watch her break her arm, and heal it, for hours on end, as he giggled, worries forgotten.

Later in life, when they were both older, he reminded her about it. *I can't believe that didn't hurt you!*

Oh, trust me, it hurt, Ana replied with a laugh.

Then why did you do it? he asked, aghast.

You needed it, she said simply.

She had never asked him for anything in return, but if Tristan could be part of giving her what she needed now, he would.

TRISTAN SHUT HIS EYES, PRETENDING TO SLEEP. INSTEAD, HE WAS looking for a telepathic connection back home. Tristan was one of the only Deschanels who could forge a telepathic link over long distance, most only being able to read those nearby, or across shorter spans. Tristan could do it from anywhere in the world, if he could find his focus.

But forging that link across a great distance was different than reading the mind of someone standing before you. It was a little like looking up at a sky full of a trillion stars, in search of the right one.

Because this was how Tristan correlated it, his mind conjured images of a vast solar system. Within it, there were many, many stars. But the stars of those he needed shined more brightly than others. And after a few minutes of stargazing, he found the star he was after: Aunt Colleen.

His mother would be upset he didn't link with her, but it took a lot of energy to keep a connection alive across such a distance and he didn't have time to filter her theatrics.

Tristan! What a relief to hear from you. I began to wonder if you'd forgotten your promise to keep us updated.

Nah. These two are a couple of wet blankets. Last time I asked for a bathroom break, Finn handed me his empty water bottle.

Finn is hurting. A lot is at stake for us, but for him, too.

Girls aren't worth the trouble.

You'll change your tune one day. Tell me, how are things going?

We've eliminated two of the four locations. On our way to the third. Fourth, if necessary, tomorrow.

There was a long pause and for a moment Tristan thought he lost the link. Then: *You will find her.*

What if we don't?

You will.

This was the real reason Tristan chose his aunt, instead of his mother. With those two words, *You will,* his shaky confidence was restored. Aunt Colleen knew what she was talking about. When she spoke, people listened. If she said they'd find Ana, they would.

We're almost there, and my head hurts. Tell my mother I love her.

Of course. And Tristan?

Yes?

You need to block extra hard. I tried earlier to pick up your thoughts and eventually broke through, for a brief moment. I'm not half the telepath you are, and you're not half the telepath those in the Senetat have access to.

Tristan's heart dropped with shame. He couldn't defend

himself against this; he knew he was being sloppy. He hadn't tried nearly hard enough. It hurt to feel like the child his mother still saw him as. *I will, Aunt C.*

We love you, Tristan. Find her, and come home to us.

I will.

"How many damn roundabouts do these people have?" Tristan grumbled, as they passed through their third. Outside the windows, snow and hills as far as the eye could see. It was starting to feel like one of those horror movies where you drove for hours, only to realize you'd gone nowhere.

"It's a form of traffic control," Finn explained, without any discernible emotion. Tristan thought it seemed like most of Finn was somewhere else, and the Finn with them was only a drop of water on the surface.

"Well, I don't think the sheep have the sophisticated brains to appreciate the gesture," Tristan mumbled, but the last of his words trailed off. Tegfynydd rose into their view, on the right, as the road turned to gravel.

Unlike the other Tudor-era castles, Tegfynydd was Victorian Gothic. Despite the differences in design from the others, Nicolas picked this one as a potential option due to the strong feeling he had about the courtyard. Tristan's skepticism deepened when he learned this. It sounded more like Nicolas was grasping at straws.

The halls stood long, and tall, with ornate designs still present and distinct, despite the obvious disrepair. It had all the high romance of Thornfield Hall in *Jane Eyre,* and, even with the weeds and vines growing around and through the windows, maintained an air of romantic sophistication.

Tristan half expected Mr. Rochester's insane wife to run out of the ruins in her tattered nightgown.

As with the prior two estates, they divided up the land. This time, Tristan was assigned the task of exploring the interior of this spooky old building, and he walked through the empty doorframe with trepidation.

It was not ghosts Tristan was fearful of encountering. He kept thinking back to Aunt Colleen's admonishment about his blocking. *Block harder.* He would, going forward. But how bare had his thoughts been until now?

Crunching through the snow sent up continuous, echoing sounds which caused the hair on his neck to stand at attention. He wished, suddenly, he had a weapon ready. His paranoid mother kept them from owning one, but he had quite a bit of practice in his first-person shooter games. He thought he could properly defend himself, if it came down to that.

Not without a weapon, though. And weapons might not even be useful against the Empyrean Senetat, who wielded abilities far more powerful than steel. There was so much they didn't know about this race they supposedly descended from. The absence of knowledge put them at an extreme disadvantage, as far as Tristan was concerned.

Tristan passed through an arching frame, half crumbled away, but the presence of a doorway was the only clue he was indoors. The roof was nonexistent, and parts of the floor had caved into the cellars, leaving a volatile pattern of snowy pathways. All furnishings had been removed at some point. As he moved through the rooms, eventually he came to a standstill before a large, stone fireplace, the chimney reaching upward and into the gray sky. A lone patch of clover grew along the top of the mantle, and as he followed the pattern above the diminutive plant, a faded, but still beautiful, mosaic came to life. He made out the distinct colors and artwork, knowing, at one point, this had been important to someone. Closing his eyes for a moment, he allowed himself to picture the house as it must have once been, many years ago.

He made it through the first floor without having a heart

attack, but when he reached the stairwell, he saw over half the stairs, leading now only to the open sky, were caved in or missing. That meant upstairs rooms would remain unexplored. *But it also means they can't be up there, right?*

Tristan hastily retreated back toward the entrance, ready to be free of the eerie building. But as he approached the central hall, he heard voices outside. He nearly ate his heart before he realized it was only Anne and Finn.

He started out to join them, until he discovered they were having a discussion he wasn't meant to hear. Grudgingly, he hung back, waiting.

"Anne, you don't know her," Finn was saying. From his vantage point, Tristan could see Anne's frustrated, flushed face, but Finn was out of sight.

"I don't need to know her to know what she did," Anne defended. She threw her hands up and out, before her. "I know this isn't what you want to hear—"

"No," Finn agreed, "it isn't. And if you felt this way, you shouldn't have come."

Tristan sensed the slow heat building inside of Anne. She said she had learned to control her ability, but it seemed to him some of the plants rustled, whistling a very subtle song.

"I came for you," Anne cried, in a voice near pleading. Her fists were balled at her sides, and her blonde hair fluttered as a small gust of wind caught it. "This won't end the way you're hoping. She chose Aidrik!"

Snow crunched as Finn shifted. "It's late. We're both tired. "

One of the willow trees bowed and swayed. Some of the vines snaking around the entrance moved almost imperceptibly. "You want to believe the best in everyone, Finn. You see the world through rose-colored glasses and I love that about you." Anne paused, blushing an even deeper shade of crimson. *She used the word love,* Tristan realized. *Finn might not have caught it, but I sure did.*

"I'm not a fool," Finn snapped. Now, the man's voice was hard. Tristan knew he should tell Anne to stop, to let it go. He had half a mind to pop out and end the conversation with an awkward entrance, but he suspected it would cause more harm than good, to get involved.

"I didn't—" Anne scrambled.

"...And I wouldn't attempt to judge your decisions, or your loved ones, based on very surface-level observations," he finished.

More snow crunched as Finn brushed past Anne, ending the conversation.

Tristan stepped out from behind the doorway. Anne's gloved fists were balled, her lips trembling. The weeds and vines before her seemed to be whispering to each other, as they swayed gently in sympathy with her angst, awaiting direction.

"You aren't going to change his mind," Tristan declared, startling her.

Anne brushed her sleeve across her face, narrowing her eyes. "And what do you know about it?"

She marched off, leaving Tristan regretting his words.

10- COLLEEN

Colleen sat before her peers at the long, oval table. It was made of the finest mahogany, imported from the West Indies by her ancestor, Charles Deschanel I. As magistrate, Colleen assumed ownership of the venerable, antique table, and it sat in a room which locked from the inside and had no keys from without. A room where secrets were made, and kept.

Colleen assumed responsibility of leading the family when her Great-aunt Ophelia passed. The burden should have passed to Charles, as the oldest, or even Augustus. But neither had stepped up, or taken much of an interest whatsoever. *You're better at it, sister,* they would say, though it was clear they couldn't have cared less if she was good at it or not.

Her five fellow Council members sat solemnly before her, their faces lit only by flickering candlelight. A total of six, where there should be seven, but that was the matter they were here to discuss.

Portraits of all the Collective magistrates stood sentry in a pattern high along the lustrous wooden paneling, as if watching from beyond. Lining all four walls, including a section covering the false door, were bookshelves, stopping barely short of the magistrate gallery, and broken up only by a large, marble hearth. A crystal chandelier hung from the tall tray ceiling, but housed only traditional candle sconces. The carpet dated back to the building of the home, and was a mosaic of red, brown, and gold floral swirls. Otherwise, there was very little decor in the room, and certainly no formal records. Those were kept in the vault, safe, and only Colleen had access.

Colleen let her eyes fall on each of her peers, one by one. First, the descendants of August: Her dearest sister, Evangeline, whose mind matched hers in nearly all matters. And her youngest sister, Elizabeth, whose presence in the Council often worried Colleen, as she feared for Elizabeth's frame of mind.

The other three were descendants of Blanche, August's sister: Jasper Broussard, a local celebrity for his work in the occult, though he delivered no more than smoke and mirrors to the public. Luther Fontenot, a wise, stoic man from a branch of the family even wealthier than some of the Deschanel heirs. He was humorless, but pragmatic, and Colleen often counted on him for support on difficult matters. Finally, the ostentatious Pansy Guidry represented the infamous Guidry clan, who were often seen as family outcasts due to some of their less than savory life choices.

The truth was, Colleen was not overly fond of Pansy or Jasper, but custom dictated the Deschanels be broadly represented in the Council. However, she wouldn't risk another Guidry or Broussard in a position of leadership. She had a perfect seventh in mind; one she was absolutely sure of. The trick would be making the others equally sure. Pansy, in particular, enjoyed the exercise of being contrary simply for the sport of it.

"Let us begin," Colleen intoned. They joined hands and solemnly chanted with her, "In power, obligation. In obligation, commitment. In commitment, solidarity. In solidarity, enlightenment." And then, the words exclusive to the Council, "In enlightenment, governance."

"Well then," Colleen began, folding her hands before her. "As you all know, we're here to discuss the induction of our seventh Council member. As the rules state, we are each allowed the opportunity to sponsor one or more nominees, and then we discuss and vote as a group."

"Why must we even press the matter of a seventh, Colleen?" Jasper asked, snapping the collar of his bismuth-pink linen suit. "It's been eight years."

"Ten," Elizabeth corrected, cheeks already aflame, though the night was early. "And if you must ask why we need a seventh member, then you clearly haven't been paying attention to the discussions about our inhuman ancestry, and how our family is in mortal danger!"

"I'm with Jasper," Pansy piped up, dropping the last consonant from each of her words in her distinct Yat dialect, "we all know you Deschanel sisters vote together, anyhow. So, whether we bring in Colleen's nominee, which we all know will happen since she always gets her way, or we continue to count her as the tie vote, ain't nothin' gonna be any different, or better."

"Please feel free to check the voting record," Evangeline replied smartly, "and you'll see your statement is incorrect. We are not always in agreement, which is precisely why we need a seventh."

"A seventh is needed, and a seventh will be added," Colleen affirmed, resuming control of her meeting. "I have two names to bring forward. If anyone else has a nominee, or nominees, please speak up now."

"I do," Pansy said, twirling her bleached hair around her pen as she gratingly smacked her spearmint gum. The sound resonated through Colleen's head; a sound she dramatically feared she would hear in her nightmares.

"I do as well," Jasper added, frowning at Pansy.

Colleen nodded. "Very well. I'll start with my first, we will listen to each of yours, and then I'll finish with my second suggestion. I'd like to propose Amelia—"

"Your daughter? You cannot be serious, what biased nonsense," Jasper charged with a dismissive flick of the wrist, looking away. He tried on a contemptuous look, but then became distracted by some lint on his cuff.

"On the contrary, Jasper, I am quite serious, and not the least bit biased. It is you who has a bias, closing your mind to her simply because she is my daughter. What are your other objections?"

"It's against the rules! No child and parent can serve at the same time, to prevent nepotism."

"Oh? Pansy and Kitty once served at the same time as their father, Pierce, before he died. And Luther's mother, Eugenia, was once on the Council as well. There was a time when I was the *only* Deschanel on the Council at all. When it was one big family reunion for Blanche's brood."

Pansy looked down at her ornate nails.

Jasper ignored her logic. "I have to agree with Pansy, you may as well leave that last spot open if this is your plan, because Amelia will always vote with her mama!" he declared, pesky lint forgotten.

"That is patently untrue," Evangeline defended, giving Jasper a look which made him retreat further into his seat. "Amelia knows her own mind, and has never been influenced by Colleen. And we are all well aware of the rules, Jasper, you don't need to remind us. The parent and child rule was put into place long after your family had already benefitted from it for years, and you know it."

"It's okay, Evie," Colleen said gently, hiding her growing frustration through a beaming smile. All this talk of rules, when there'd been almost none when Colleen took over as magistrate.

Despite knowing they would reject Amelia's nomination,

and that actually being her desired outcome, she found herself irritated with her cousins, as she often was. "They've a right to their concerns. Let's move on to Pansy's suggestion now."

Pansy brightened at the opportunity to give her opinion, something she placed great stock in. Colleen thought, not for the first time, Pansy wore her blonde hair big and tall to give the impression her thoughts were equally substantial. Colleen was not fooled.

"Why, my little sister, Kitty, has been asking for *years* to come back," Pansy began, but Luther put a hand up before she could speak another word.

"Lord in heaven, no. We've discussed this. One Guidry on this damned Council is enough. If she wanted to come back, she shouldn't have left to begin with," he barked. Colleen had to hide a smile at seeing Luther's normally unruffled countenance turn flustered.

"Amen," Elizabeth mumbled.

Pansy looked mortally offended, and opened her mouth to counter when Jasper spoke up.

"My sister, Imogen. She more than fits the criteria."

Colleen nodded thoughtfully, surprised to hear a legitimate suggestion. Imogen Dubois was not a bad choice. She was not the least bit like her pandering brother, and she'd married into a good family, one who hardly raised an eyebrow at the Deschanel craziness. But Colleen's mind was set on a different course, so she would let this play out until it was her turn again.

"Certainly worth considering," she replied, careful to balance her support with enough hesitation.

"Hmph," replied Pansy, as if that was all the objection needed.

Silence, as she allowed the others to process that nomination, knowing they would take her own response as apprehension. This was what she wanted. Amelia had merely been a diversion; a clever battle tactic. She'd anticipated they would veto her induction, and she also knew that would make them more amenable to her final suggestion. Being magistrate often involved a great deal of strong leadership, and occasionally, manipulation.

She wasn't fond of deception, but viewed her role as deciding what was the best for the Council, and the family. This responsibility was always at the front of her mind.

"Colleen, who is your last nominee?" Luther asked.

"Nicolas," Colleen replied, after a reasonable pause. She added nothing, waiting for the air to be sucked from the room as her fellow Council fought to voice their objections. She was not disappointed.

"Colleen, we all agreed the heir cannot be a Council Member. After Charles," Luther reminded evenly. Charles had been boastful and controlling, often sidetracking their meetings, insisting, as the heir, his vote held more weight. He lasted no more than a year, and after his death they all voted to prevent similar derailing in the future.

"Nicolas won't be the heir much longer," Colleen countered. "He has passed that honor to Anasofiya, and her son, Aleksandr. He is entirely free to become one of us—"

"He's a jackass," Pansy snorted, before Colleen could finish her thought. "He doesn't even take any of this seriously!"

"He does now," Colleen replied. "And he's possibly the strongest Deschanel living, now that he has come into his powers. Additionally, as the son of our Charles, he should be represented."

"He is also," Evangeline added, "our only solid link to Ana, and by extension, Aidrik. And the Empyreans. That link is vital to our understanding, and survival, as we seek answers. He's representing our entirely family in this. Do we really want him to do it without our guidance and support?"

"He is absolutely not even an option," Pansy declared, leaning back, arms spread along the length of her velvet chair.

Her well-coiffed hair did not move even an inch as her head bobbed around. "When did we decide this Council was a circus?"

Elizabeth smirked knowingly, tossing an eye roll at her sisters as if to say, *Can you believe this chick?*

"Pansy," Colleen pushed, calmly, "please give me one objective reason why Nicolas is not an option."

"*Colleen*," Pansy condescended, "give us one objective reason why he *is*."

"I believe she provided several very salient ones," Luther spoke up, silencing his cousin with both words and glance. He then looked toward Colleen, dismissing Pansy altogether. "Has Nicolas expressed an interest?"

Colleen nodded. "He has, and with the project he's sponsoring with Mercy, for the Runean refugees, these discussions will become necessary for him. It does neither him, nor us, any good for him to be in the dark. These discussions cannot be mutually exclusive."

"I support Nicolas," Luther replied, his strong jaw was set tight. His steel-gray eyes pierced each of them, squelching the objections sitting on their tongues. "As should all of you. Using your emotions as a guide here will only waste valuable time. The landscape has changed, and we must adapt. I'm sure outlining the alternative is unnecessary."

Colleen flashed a brief, but very grateful, look at her cousin. He didn't return it, but she thought she saw a small glint in his eye as he trained his gaze on her from his peripheral. "And there is no worry of perceived nepotism with Nicolas. No one has ever accused him of following the pack. That objection can be put to bed."

The debate continued over the mahogany table, but the shared looks between Colleen and Luther were the knowing kind, one which said the argument was won and they need only be patient. *Everyone accuses Evangeline and Elizabeth of being in agreement with me, but my real ally in this room has always been Luther.*

Within the hour, it was decided. Nicolas would be the seventh member, assuming he passed their usual line of questioning. *And not a moment too soon. If I cannot persuade him to reach his potential, then perhaps the others can. The Senetat threat is very real and his full participation will undoubtedly make a difference.*

NICOLAS SAT IN THE SEVENTH SEAT, LOOKING LIKE THE CHILD HE'D never truly been. His chestnut eyes were wide and curious, his cheeks pale. His dark hair, curled at the temples from nervous sweat, looked as if he'd been running his hands through it all night. He kept glancing up at the magistrate portraits warily as if he expected them to jump out of the frame and strangle him.

Colleen wished for a moment they were alone so she could tease him, or even offer reassurance, but they were not, and they had important business to attend to.

"Nicolas, we've all agreed to consider you as the candidate, but each of the Council now has the right to ask you questions designed to determine your fit and potential," Colleen explained. "Realizing patience is not one of your strong suits, I'd ask you to employ what little you do possess, and bear with us."

"Understood," Nicolas replied, shifting nervously. His usual smirk was notably absent.

"My first question is, why are you interested in a Council position?" Evangeline began.

Nicolas sat forward in his seat, leaning over his folded hands. "The past few months have been rather... illuminating. It's going to be one hell of a rollercoaster going forward, and I could really use some partnership before stepping over the edge into God knows what. What's happening now affects all of us."

Colleen's lip twitched into a small smile. She knew he must

have practiced some humility before coming in. It gave her hope, to see how much he'd grown up in recent days. "No doubt of that," she agreed, nodding.

Pansy dropped her pen, with a bit more force than was required, and stopped smacking her gum. "Bull honky! You *never* attend family events and have never cared about any of this before. How do we know you will risk your spoiled hiney to protect the family the rest of us holds so sacred?"

Nicolas' smirk finally made an appearance. "I can see family is important to you, Pansy. The Guidry tree never did have many branches..."

She sat up straight, aghast. "You are one to talk, making out with your sister, Anne!"

"I didn't know she was my sister at the time!"

"We're not going to indulge this kind of pettiness," Luther said, fixing his sturdy gaze on Pansy. "Nicolas, please address the first part of her question, regarding the importance of family."

"*Couillon*," Pansy muttered, under her breath.

Nicolas squared his shoulders, shooting an insolent wink Pansy's direction before answering. "You're right. I didn't much give a shit before now. Why should I have? You knew my father." At this, several nodded sadly, remembering his childhood neglect. "But things are different now. Ana, who I love more than anyone in this world, is having a child soon, and that child will be my heir. That matters to me."

"You've always been so good to her, dear," Evangeline agreed, patting a hand over his.

"So ask me anything you like," Nicolas finished. "I promise I won't lose sleep over your opinion of me, and I can't pretend I'm not going to continue to be an asshole when the mood strikes. It's genetic. But my intentions relating to the Council are pure."

The Council took their turns drilling Nicolas with their

questions. To Colleen's great relief, he didn't lose his composure even once, answering each of their inquiries with a calm rationale she hadn't thought him capable of. He endured the exercise with great patience, and humility.

"And how good are you with secrets? You can't go telling that friend of yours. That Oz Sullivan," Jasper interjected, as they finished up. He raised an eyebrow, as if expecting Nicolas to go straight to Oz's after the meeting.

Nicolas gave a light shrug. "Eh, he already knows. And not because I told him."

"Most of the Sullivans know," Evangeline reminded Jasper. "They're not just the Deschanel attorneys, but they also represent us, the Collective. You know that."

"Not to mention, one is my husband," Elizabeth added.

Jasper nodded, as if he already knew, and didn't like it one bit.

"Besides," Elizabeth said, "the Sullivans aren't exactly benign, either. More than once I've seen Connor slide the ketchup across the table when I didn't pass it quick enough. And don't even get me started on Rory's mind tricks!"

Everyone in the room look surprised by this, except Colleen. She'd known the Sullivans had subtle abilities of their own, though they went to great pains to squash them, as if they were ashamed, or thought them bad for business.

No one raised additional objections, and silence slowly filled the room. Colleen sighed inwardly in relief. All questions had been answered to the satisfaction of the Council. Even Pansy's.

"There is one last thing," Colleen said with a tentative glance at Evangeline, who was the only other person who knew what she had planned. The rest of the Council looked as taken aback as Nicolas. *This is not my preferred method of handling things, but I fear it's the only way.* "Before our inductions, each of us fully explored the depth of our abilities. I believe there are parts of yours you have been hesitant to uncover. We must know what they are before we allow you in."

"Aunt C—"

"No," she interrupted. "This is not negotiable, Nicolas. You have these powers for a reason. We need to know what it is. This is not simply about the mission we've sent Anne, Tristan, and Finn on. This is about our family's fate."

"Dammit kiddo, what she's trying to say is, we think your visions aren't bullshit. They're prophetic," Elizabeth exclaimed, her face again flushed in clear exasperation.

"We need to know you're not afraid to explore them. And use them, if and when they're needed," Evangeline finished.

A broad smile spread across Nicolas' face. "Oh, is that all?" Before Colleen could deduce his vague meaning, her nephew closed his eyes and drew in a deep breath. Both hands clutched the sides of his chair as a new, concentrated energy collected around him. Not visible, but she could feel it. And she could see the others did, too.

Then, his eyes flew open. He looked toward Pansy at the other end of the table. No, past her. His eyes fixed on a corner of the bookshelf, as he cocked his head. Then he grinned, as if stumbling into an old friend. The rest of the room followed his gaze, but saw only books and oak.

Realization slowly dawned on Colleen. *He's done it. He's pulled a seer's vision from Aidrik, on his own. Awake. The little brat listened to me after all.*

Then, with a beaming smile, Nicolas said, "This vision is *much* less disturbing Aidrik, thank you."

11- FINN

The drive to Gwynfryn Castle, their last hope, was long and windy. Outside, snowy hills and valleys were covered in a thick mist, as far as the eye could see.

They started out from their small inn in Carmarthenshire, after a breakfast none of them touched. Tristan made some effort to move the fruit across his plate, but Finn hadn't even unfolded his napkin and utensils. Anne didn't bother joining them at all.

She was angry, and while he recognized it had to do with him, Finn was having trouble understanding exactly *why*.

The night before, they were all exhausted and moody as they said their goodbyes and went to their respective rooms. But Anne had, at the last minute, jogged to catch up with Finn.

We have a long drive ahead of us tomorrow, he'd said. The words would serve either as a helpful reminder, or a gentle admonishment, depending on her intentions.

The baby robin, she said suddenly. Her voice was rushed, as if unsure whether she should stay them at all.

Sorry?

How we met, her words were emphatic. *The baby robin out in the gardens of* Ophélie. *Do you remember?*

Finn remembered. He'd come upon a baby robin fallen from its nest, quite high in the tree. Then Anne came along and used her special talents to lower the branch, so Finn could restore the little bird to his home.

He nodded, confused as to her intended point.

That's why I care, she said. Her face flushed. *Most people would have looked up at that branch and said, ah well, that's too high. But not you. You looked at it as if you might climb the damn thing if you had to. And if I hadn't come along, I think you might have.*

I'm sure I could have had one of the house staff find a ladder...

But Anne had shaken her head vigorously. *The point is, most people would have given up. They would have put that poor bird down and gone on with their life. You didn't. I knew then you were something pretty damn special, Finnegan St. Andrews. Special people deserve good things.*

Finn had never thought of the things that happened in life as stuff he deserved or didn't. His father, the esteemed Dr. St. Andrews, had taught Finn, and his brother Jon, that anything in life worth wanting was worth working for. And so Finn had worked hard, every single day of his life. He'd labored, and those labors had borne fruit. He didn't believe he *deserved* anything. If he wanted it, he would have to go after it. Just as he was doing now.

Thank you, he said finally. *It's late—*

Then, she had shocked them both by taking his hand in hers, firmly, clasping it between her two tiny ones. *You deserve so much more.*

Finn had pulled his hand back, with a gentle tug. He realized, at that moment, Anne's feelings for him had grown past a hopeful, future affection, into unrequited love. He drew in a sad breath, and sighed. In an awareness born of his own loss, he didn't want to hurt her, but couldn't give her what she wanted.

The only thing I want lies at the end of our journey tomorrow, he clarified, as kindly as he could. *If you're not up to it, I'll understand if you want to stay behind. Tristan can get you on the way back to the airport.*

Tristan? What about you?

I'm not coming home, he said.

She changed then, before his eyes. She went from being mournful to proud, the latter quickly erasing any trace of the former. Her eyes seemed brighter, her posture erect. *She's willing herself to feel better,* he realized.

No, she said, head held high, *I will help you.* And with that, she turned on her heels and strode back down the long hall toward her room.

But she'd punished him with her defection at breakfast, and she was punishing him now with the silent gazes out into the vast snowy landscape.

He had never once led her to believe they could be anything other than friends. But, he couldn't exactly begrudge her for her feelings, either. She could no more help hers than he could help his.

Throughout the drive, Finn thought a lot about how he would feel when he saw Ana again, but had given very little attention to what he would say. He understood his actions would speak loudest, and anyway he was usually better at coming up with words in the moment. He was likely to fumble them, prepared or not.

Finn pictured Ana's long, beautiful red hair. Remembered how it sparkled against the breaking sun, under the Maine sky. The way her smile lit up her entire face, creasing her thoughtful blue eyes. He wished he could say he had the foresight, then, to know how much he would come to love her. But in those first moments, she had left a lasting impact.

Mercy had explained to Finn about this so-called evigbond which had driven Ana into Aidrik's arms. That the bond was uncommon, but also unseverable. *She has no choice in the matter,* Mercy had said. *She is his, and he is hers, until the day one of them perishes from the Earth.* Well, maybe that was true. But if Empyreans had evigbond, then humans had something just as strong. Just as potent, and real, and unbreakable. Ana may be part Empyrean, but she was also part human. And her human part loved Finn.

"I talked to Aunt C again," Tristan spoke up, from the backseat, peeling his earbuds out.

"Again?" Anne asked. She'd missed Tristan catching Finn up at breakfast. "When?"

"Just now, while you were pouting."

Finn kept his focus on the road, listening.

"Well, what did she say?" Anne demanded.

"Nicolas has been in contact with Aidrik, who has been sharing his seer's visions." Tristan paused, and Finn thought he was doing it to goad her on. It was working. "Some were good, some were not."

"Are you going to tell us, or what?" she snapped.

Tristan ignored her and leaned up toward Finn. "Do you wanna pull over? You might not wanna hear this while you're driving."

Finn's heart seized in his chest. He swerved, then forced his mind back to the present, maneuvering the car over into a gravel turnabout. *Do you want to pull over?* The equivalent of, *You might want to sit down.* Reserved for moments when you needed to break the absolute worst of news. The words his father had used when his mother passed on. The same words, years later, the doctors employed when Andrew St. Andrews also passed.

"Tell me," Finn said. Beside him, Anne's eyes were wide, as she looked back and forth between both men, in anxious concern.

"First, the good news. I think we're headed to the right place. Aidrik could find no signs announcing where they were, and he didn't wanna leave Ana, but he projected to Nicolas a general location which seems to be where we're going," Tristan said brightly, with a forced look of hopefulness plastered on his face.

"That isn't exactly more than what we had before. It's either right or wrong, and if wrong, we're back to the start anyway," Anne sighed. "What else?"

"Ana is sick. She's getting worse," Tristan confided hesitantly, looking both guilty and distressed at being the messenger of such news. "And Aidrik is growing more and more worried she might not make it."

"Might not..." Finn repeated the words in his mind, but they didn't sound any more real than when Tristan spoke them. He closed his eyes, slowly inhaling. "Go on."

"She's rail thin, except her distortedly swollen belly. The skin over it is bruised purple. She's refusing food. Aidrik heals her daily, and she heals herself, but the troubles with her body aren't the worst of it. He thinks she's shutting down emotionally, which is preventing her from accepting the healing fully. When she sleeps..."

"When she sleeps what, Tristan?" Anne pressed. The venom from earlier was gone, and her face had gone pale.

Tristan looked at Finn. "She calls out for you."

Finn turned from them and looked out at the road ahead. At the end of it, Ana was waiting. For him. He wasn't wrong. *He wasn't wrong.*

All of his emotions—all the love, worry, sickness, regret, pain, passion—rushed forward inside him all at once, erupting in the form of gasping, choked sobs.

Finn buried his face in his hands and cried.

12- ANNE

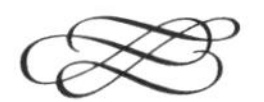

Anne's heart was bruised. At first, it had been a very selfish sensation, of knowing there was nothing she could say or do to show Finn he need not traipse around in search of a woman who had left him, seemingly without remorse. He need only look in front of him to find a woman who was willing to give *all* of herself. A woman who would not make him second choice, and would never, ever make him share her heart.

Then, the feeling evolved. Not slowly, either. The evolution culminated in the very moment Tristan revealed Ana did, in fact, love Finn. That she, right this moment even, was likely regretting her decision to leave him. And Ana was paying a price for it, as Finn was.

Anne suspected there were things Tristan held back from Finn, out of kindness or on order from Aunt Colleen. Likely both. Anne worried they might be running out of time faster than they originally thought. They might arrive too late. She now, finally, understood there was nothing naive about Finn's love, or about the very real possibility Ana might die before he could reunite with her.

She wanted desperately to talk to Tristan, but she didn't want to do it in the presence of Finn. The man was unyielding as a rock, no doubt, but he was barely holding it together. His white knuckles and clenched jaw illustrated this, in case there was any doubt.

"So beautiful," Anne said, looking out the window at the Snowdonia mountain range, covered in drifting snow. It wasn't a brilliant contribution to the silence, but the tension in the car was so thick she had to say something, or scream.

"Definitely not shit we see back home," Tristan agreed.

This was followed by more silence. There simply wasn't anything that could be said with such weighty things looming over them.

Anne decided, with some uncertainty, to break the news she had been keeping to herself all this time. Colleen would be ashamed if she knew *why* Anne had kept quiet: she was hoping Finn would change his mind.

"If Ana agrees to marry you," she began tentatively, looking at Finn, "I can help."

Finn flashed her a sidelong glance but said nothing.

"When I was growing up in the bayou, I was trained to do a lot of things. Most of them unofficially, like midwifery," she went on. "But our bayou community was tight-knit. The only non-denominational church had a single pastor."

Tristan had put down his iPod and was listening, rapt. Finn had also relaxed his grip on the steering wheel.

"When he fell ill, our community scrambled to find people to fill his shoes. One of the elders in the church took over sermons. Another assumed responsibility for community outreach." Anne took a deep breath, swallowing. *You care for him. He's suffering. You can help.* "Several of us stepped up and offered to be ordained to officiate important ceremonies. Baptisms, Sunday Service. For me, it was marriages."

Finn looked at her quickly, before returning his eyes to the road. Tristan leaned forward and mocked, "So you got one of those back-of-the-magazine certificates which says you can marry people?"

Anne's eyes narrowed. Super telepath or not, her younger cousin was obnoxious. "No, not from the back of a *magazine*. Ordained through the church. By God."

Tristan scoffed at this, but leaned further forward. "Sorry, we're all failed Catholics in this family. We'd likely be smote down by God Himself if we stepped through the doors of a church. What about you, Finn? What do you believe?"

Finn frowned, twisting his lips together. "I don't know anymore." As he said this, his hand traveled up to his neck, where he pulled out two crosses, linked together.

Finn shifted his peripheral gaze to Anne. "You're saying you can marry us?"

Anne nodded. The tears welled in her throat, but she swallowed them down. She was stronger and better than the foolish girl she'd paraded herself as. Maybe she couldn't help her feelings, but she could control her behavior. "Yes, I can."

Finn let out a sigh which seemed to last minutes. "Shit. I hadn't even *thought* about that. In all this, it didn't occur to me we would need someone to actually *perform* the ceremony." He tensed his jaw again, and Anne thought maybe he was fighting back tears of his own. "Thank you, Anne," he whispered. "Thank you, thank you, thank you."

Anne nodded. "Thank me when we get there. Now, does this car go any faster, or what?"

13- AIDRIK

Evening stretched into morning, and then into afternoon. Anasofiya continued her restless sleep. Aidrik would wake her and insist she take food, but anytime she did, she would only retch it back up. Aidrik loathed this helplessness. Not knowing how to help her weighed on his soul. He did not know where her physical hurts ended and her emotional ones began.

Within the brick walls of the old manor, they were protected from the elements, but it had started to snow again. He stoked the fire, knowing the chill would soon find them. Outside, the wind gusted off the mountainous landscape to where they sat in the open valley of weeds and ruination. The east wing was mostly intact, other than the half-gaping sky above, but brick and stone did not entirely shield them from the cold. Where tapestries would have hung in older days to insulate the inhabitants, they had nothing but their own warmth, and what little the fire offered.

Aidrik was not cold, though. Empyrean bodies ran hotter than Men, and their homeland, Farjhem, lay in the northern glaciers of Norway. He was built for the cold, and designed to withstand it.

Anasofiya's shivering bothered him. He had believed the Sveising made her full Empyrean. Before, of course, she had been a Halfling. All Deschanels were. The Sveising was such an unpredictable process, and employing it on a Child of Man, even if she was a Halfling, seemed a great risk. But after, she was brighter. Better. Faster. All of her abilities were amplified. She had become a resurrection shaman, an ability rare even among Empyreans. Her skin grew warmer to the touch, and her fiery hair and eyes-like-the-sea took on an elevated vibrancy.

Am I Empyrean now? she had asked. *I believe so,* he had said. He would not have answered with such confidence had he not possessed it. But now... now as she lay shivering, and possibly dying, he wondered if he had severely miscalculated things.

Their son, Aleksandr—the son of all three of them: Finn, Anasofiya, and Aidrik—was undoubtedly full Empyrean. Aidrik knew simply by laying his hands on her swollen belly, and sensing his son's presence through the flesh and bone. *That should have been your first indication she was unwell. You should have sensed it in her, too, and didn't.*

He could not dwell overlong on such missteps. Aidrik had never put much stock in regret. It was a waste of energy to focus on the past, when the future required your full presence.

Aidrik looked again at the tattered sweatshirt she wore. It was large, unshapely, and frayed, made for a man's frame. In the center, a faded fleur de lis, barely discernible.

Before leaving Louisiana, he had taken Anasofiya to her home to pack a small bag. She had few items in her bureau suited for colder climes, so she'd pulled out some jeans, and this old sweatshirt from where it was shoved into the bottom of a box at the rear of her closet. It looked entirely unlike anything his Anasofiya would wear, and he couldn't help venturing forward with the question of where it had come from.

The look in her eyes had been faraway when she responded, not as if remembering her own life, so much as recalling a story she'd once read and loved. *It belonged to an old friend. An old love. Oz,* she'd told him. *Back from a time when things were much simpler.*

When Aidrik prodded in wonder at why she would hold on to such a derelict garment, she had replied, *Sometimes it's good to hold on to a piece of who you were. There's a hope in remembering. You might yet become the person you always tried to be.*

Aidrik had nothing for her in response. He would not have believed Anasofiya capable of such sentiment. But if it was a part of who she was, he would learn to accept, and embrace it.

SNOW SWIRLED THROUGH A CRACK IN THE BRICK, AND ANASOFIYA woke. Immediately, her eyes fixed on Aidrik's. His heart swelled, to see her so alert, though he wondered what brought it on.

"Are you well-rested, *Kjære?*" he asked. He reached a hand to her forehead. Hot. Not the kind of heat he wanted.

She slipped her hands under her, pushing herself to a half-sitting, half-leaning position. Her red hair was pinned to the side of her face, and her lips were chalky. Dry. "As much as I can expect to be, I suppose," she replied in a hoarse voice.

Aidrik placed his hands against her belly, where his son grew ever fast. Though he longed to meet him, he couldn't help but wonder if, in the end, he would need to choose. *Aleksandr or Anasofiya.* It would not be an easy choice, but he would choose her. Always her. *My evigbond.*

"Soon now," he encouraged, with a cracked smile. He struggled to project the cheerfulness he thought she needed, when he felt none. "Then I can restore your health fully."

She returned his smile, but it was hollow, like her eyes. "If I make it that long," she replied, in a tone meant to be teasing.

"You will," he assured her. But what he didn't say was, *If I have to choose, I will,* Kjære. *I would mourn the loss of our son. But I would not survive the loss of you.*

"What do we have to eat?" she asked. Aidrik's heart swelled at this; the first time she had asked for food in days.

Anticipating this day might come, he had slain a lamb from a nearby farm. She had not been able to keep down the rodents, and required something of more substance in her condition.

Anasofiya devoured the lamb with vigor, though Aidrik had to caution her to go slowly. "Your stomach is empty," he reminded her.

When she finished, some of the color returned to her face. She leaned against the cold wall, Aidrik's woolen cloak pulled over her. In the dancing flames of the fire, she looked more beautiful than anything he had ever seen, in all his wanderings.

"Aidrik," she said, after a companionable silence, a dreamy expression clouding her face, her hair swimming around her like a blazing halo. He felt a stirring under his trousers, which abashed him. Physical connection was how Anasofiya forged her bonds, because she knew no better. She had indoctrinated him, and now his thoughts were no longer his own.

"Yes, *Kjære?*"

"I know you can hear my thoughts when my guard is down. When I'm dreaming," she replied.

"I can," he affirmed. If she wished to have this discussion, he welcomed it. Better that than let it continue to linger over them like a dark storm cloud.

"And you don't understand," she finished.

He slid across the dusty stone floor, and moved in beside her. "I understand well enough. You love him."

"I love you," she replied, in a voice near insisting.

"You love us both," he corrected. "Your bond to me is sacred. Your bond to him is of the soul."

Her eyes widened in surprise. He saw this thought had not occurred to her. *All this time she has been punishing herself.*

"I made a choice when I left," she said. Her hand clutched Aidrik's leg, attempting to prop herself up higher. "I don't know how to fix it."

Aidrik chuckled. The rare sound reverberated through the cold stone. "This is where we are very different. It is your upbringing, as a Child of Man, which tells you your heart can love only one person. From a race who conveniently forgot marriage started out as no more than a legal arrangement."

She tried to speak, but he continued. "I do not fault you, or loathe you, or think less of you for loving us both, *Kjære.* And I wish you would stop tormenting yourself over your own humanity. A whole life you have lived, doing it. Self-loathing is unnecessary." *And it hurts me to see you thus.*

"But my humanity is everything to me," she replied. "I understand your point, but people don't share well." She dropped her eyes. "I couldn't bear to see you hold another woman."

"You needn't trouble yourself," he said drily. "As long as you live, my evigbond, I could not take another even if I desired it."

But silently, to himself only, Aidrik recalled the current situation had not been her choice at all. It had been his, through his power of influence. Applying it only when she refused to leave Finn, he believed he was doing right by her. Now, he was no longer so certain. Worse, he felt incapable of revealing his deception, for fear of making her condition worse. Of driving her further from his arms.

After Aleksandr is born. I will tell her then, and she can decide what to do with the confession. Even if I lose her.

"When I'm resting, I focus on Aleksandr. On making him strong, and seeing him born into this world," his Anasofiya said, running both hands over her belly. "I want him to be all that matters, but I know better. To love him the way he deserves, it's impossible not to love myself. And to love myself, I have to know who I am, and stop pretending I'll ever be anyone else. I'm not the silly girl I once was, losing her head over things that, in hindsight, didn't even matter. I know now I'm not a terrible person, and this darkness inside me... how to explain it..."

"It is not the weakness you perceived it to be," Aidrik offered.

"Yes," she agreed, nodding. "Without it, I might have given up years ago. I can embrace it, in the same way I pushed it away before. I understand now it's the piece of myself that makes me resilient, and whole." She paused. "I *want* to live, Aidrik. The words sound so... simple. But they mean something when I say them now. And it isn't just Aleksei driving these feelings. This isn't some newfound maternal longing pushing me forward blindly. It's *me*. I'm not who I was before."

Aidrik said nothing. The words she spoke now were the most she'd uttered since he brought her here. It was a joyful realization, to learn her weeks of rest were filled with self-reflection.

Anasofiya leaned forward then. Her matted hair fell over her face as she hovered near the fire, flame upon flame dancing before him. A goddess of fire. "In fact, I'm *better,*" she finished. "I'm alive. For the first time."

"Undoubtedly so," Aidrik replied, with a reassuring smile. "And it is refreshing to hear the words come from you."

Settling back again, Anasofiya's glow dampened slightly. Once back in the shadows, she frowned. "But in spite of all that, I feel as if an integral piece of me is missing," she said, carefully. "If what you say about the evigbond is true, then why do I still love him *this much*? Why can't I put it behind me?"

Aidrik shook his head. "My supposition is you retain enough Man to follow both paths." *Truth later, when she is stronger.*

"I didn't tell you this, though I suppose there's still a lot you don't know about me," she went on, not addressing his theory, "but something awful happened to me right before we met. Someone I trusted hurt me. Finn's brother." A shadow passed over her face then, but it was not the shadows he was used to seeing. This one read more like rage than sadness. "What he did to me was disgraceful. It was horrible. But worst of all was the power I let him have over me. I allowed him to let me believe I somehow welcomed his attack, that I deserved it. And then I let him drive me away from Finn."

Aidrik made a mental note to annihilate Finn's brother if ever their paths should cross. But he did not interrupt.

She continued, "I think about that day a lot. I wonder if I could've fought him harder, or said or done something differently, to cause a better outcome. But no matter how many endings I try to imagine, the only satisfying one concludes with me standing over him, blood on my hands." Anasofiya closed her eyes. "But it isn't him I see dead. It's the part of me that let him hurt me. The part that bought into his belief I wasn't good enough for Finn, and didn't deserve him. The me who let others have power over me they didn't deserve."

"*Kjære*, it is beyond my power to correct your belief," Aidrik said gently.

"It's been corrected," Anasofiya replied, with a firm set of her mouth and brows. "'The exquisite pain,' Jon said to me, before he tried to rape me. He wanted me to understand how he felt about wanting something he couldn't have, as if his hurt somehow exonerated him. But I understand the words, now, more than he ever could. The exquisite pain..."

Aidrik realized what she was trying to tell him, but needed her to say it. It was important she get it out.

"I love Finn," Anasofiya said plainly, meeting Aidrik's eyes. "I shouldn't have left him, Aidrik. You told me it was to protect him, but even then I knew it was a weak excuse. I was still punishing myself, because it was all I knew how to do." She slipped a hand over Aidrik's in gentle companionship. "When Aleksandr is born, I'm going to go in search of his father. I'm sure he's hurt and angry, and he might even hate me, which is his right after all that's happened. But if he loves me as I believe he does, he will understand. And if I have to, I will fight for him, as he has for me."

Now that it was all in the open, Aidrik felt an inexplicable sense of relief. When she would waffle back and forth about her intentions, torturing herself, he found it impossible to reach her, or help her. This resolved, confident Anasofiya gave him a sense of purpose. They could move forward. He embraced absolutes.

"If this is your wish, I will help you accomplish it," Aidrik responded.

"Thank you," she said. The wind outside whipped around the stones, creating a thundering effect. The fire flickered ever so slightly, as the musty smell of the castle wafted up through slight cracks in the walls.

Anasofiya shivered, but did not retreat. "I love you also, you know. It's not just because of this evigbond. I mean, it might have been at first." She smiled, and this time the look flattered her. He couldn't help returning it. "But you're more to me than some chemical process I can't comprehend. We understand one another, Aidrik. In a way no one else could ever understand us."

He nodded. "Aye. A surprise to both of us."

"I don't know what it will mean for us. I still have some thinking to do."

Aidrik understood all she didn't say, as well. Any reassurances he could give would be ineffective.

But her new, more truthful view of herself heartened him. She wasn't afraid anymore. No longer riddled with false guilt. Nothing he could offer her would mean more than the gift she had given herself.

Aidrik wrapped his arms around her, pulling her gently into his lap. He did not stroke her hair, or caress her cheek, as Finn might. Instead, he loved her by giving her his silent, steeled strength and warmth.

All he could do now was hope the visions he shared with Nicolas would bear fruit.

14- TRISTAN

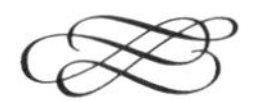

When they were within five kilometers of Gwynfryn, Tristan felt a certainty creep up within him his cousin was near. And it had nothing to do with Aunt Colleen telling him Nicolas saw mountains, and a bay, in his most recent visions, both of which Tristan could now see before them.

Though a telepath couldn't read the mind of those blocking the intrusion, there were still certain things the senses picked up. Tristan thought of them as echoes. Thoughts and actions left behind; suggestions of evidence. As they approached the estate, he very distinctly began to feel traces of Ana's echoes.

He didn't dare say this to Finn or Anne, though. They both wore intense looks of determination on their tired faces, each for very different reasons, and he feared they might join forces to tear his head off if he was wrong. But he wasn't wrong. He might dread how they would *receive* the message, but he didn't doubt the accuracy of his senses.

All at once Tristan wished for his mother. She was irrational, and emotional, and often embarrassed him, but she was still his mother. He felt very alone in this cold country, despite the company beside him.

"Just up there," Anne directed, pointing toward the road ahead as she glanced down at the map. Yes, Tristan's sense of the echoes grew stronger with every turn of the wheel. With it, his fear of what they might find. "The road seems to stop at that inn. We can park there."

As Finn maneuvered the car down the narrow road, Tristan's mind continued to race. What if this Aidrik, this Viking warrior, flashed his steel and decapitated them in one swift move? Tristan hadn't had the pleasure of meeting the ancient bloke, but from all accounts Aidrik was a "slice first, ask questions later" type. It wouldn't take much to bring this fellowship to a swift end.

One more thing for me to dwell on in a long list of crap I'm already worried about.

As they approached the inn, Anne gripped the top of the car door, and the window began to rattle in its frame. Tristan realized she sensed it, too. And then Finn surprised them both by throwing the car into neutral and wrenching up the parking brake, before launching into a full sprint down the winding footpath ahead. *The castle must be in the middle of that thicket.* Tristan supposed even ordinary men, like Finn, could sense things when they meant enough.

Tristan removed the keys and struggled to catch up with Anne, who chased behind Finn. As they followed him, panting, the trees grew denser, and his doubts crept in. *There can't possibly be anything in here,* he thought. But then the trail opened up into a large field, littered with old artifacts long since devoured by the consuming foliage. And, in the center, stood an old rundown mansion. The sight before them was as depressing as the circumstances that brought them there.

"*Ana!*" Finn screamed into the crisp air, not stopping to look. He hurled himself toward the crumbling estate, tripping over rocks and rogue pieces of machinery. Old automobile engines, plow apparatus, and discarded furniture protruded from the snow, alongside the tall brown weeds. This was a graveyard for the unwanted.

Tristan nearly tripped himself, trying to follow after him, but Anne forestalled his progress with a hand on his shoulder. "Let him go. She's here."

"I know," Tristan snapped, wrenching free of her. "I could've told you that ten minutes ago."

"Why didn't you?" Anne asked with a lift of her eyebrow. She marched after Finn, but maintained a respectable distance.

In his haste, Finn had forgotten to close off his thoughts. They were now coming to Tristan in a flood: *Dear God, please let her be okay, I'll do anything, please, I cannot live without her.*

The sound of hundreds of tiny wings overwhelmed them, as pigeons came hurling out of the brick ruins, scattering in all directions. Then, a tiny voice echoing in the distance: "Finn!"

"Ana!"

Tristan and Anne forgot all pretense of giving the couple privacy and sprinted to catch up, tripping through tall weeds and shrubs, as they fought to finally lay eyes upon victory.

As their path opened into a courtyard, Tristan saw her: Ana. Her body appeared rudely disproportionate in her final weeks of pregnancy, but her face erupted in the most confusing flow of emotions Tristan had ever seen. And then she discarded her heavy woolen cloak and ran toward Finn with an unexpected vigor, her arms out. Finn knelt down and opened his arms, receiving her into a crushing embrace.

Tristan had only seen things like this in the movies. Beside him, Anne gasped.

"Finn, oh God, you're here, you silly man," Ana cried, her face buried in the younger man's neck. "My Poseidon. I'm sorry, I'm so sorry, my God, you're really here, you're really really here."

"Silly girl," Finn whispered. Tristan also heard: *Be strong for her. You have to. She needs it.* "I told you I would always follow wherever you went."

Finn broke from the embrace and cradled her face in his hands, studying her as if he hadn't laid eyes on her in a hundred years. From where Tristan stood, he could see his cousin's face burst into the silent, open-mouthed sob of a child. It was the most heart-wrenching thing he had ever witnessed.

"I'm here," Finn repeated, choking her sob with a firm, possessive kiss. "I'm here."

Ana launched into a slew of jumbled, fractured questions, but Finn silenced each of them with his own desperate reassurances. *Be strong,* Tristan heard him reminding himself, but his thoughts would fly back to the realization Ana was back in his arms, and she hadn't sent him away. *She called out for me.*

"He really loves her," Anne remarked. She didn't sound sad so much as aware. Knowing and seeing were two very different things.

"He does," Tristan agreed.

"And she loves *him,*" Anne added, as if making a great realization. Her voice tilted at the end with wonder, as she watched them with a spreading curiosity.

"Love doesn't mean a damn thing if you're a Deschanel," Tristan told her. "The whole family is cursed. Getting attached to anyone is asking for trouble, for both you and them." Without meaning to, he sounded exactly like his mother.

Anne swiped at the few rogue tears pooling in her eyes. "You don't really believe that, do you?"

"Yes," Tristan replied sadly, as he watched two lovers reunite; two souls who were meant to be joined. "I really do."

15- FINN

Though Finn had given a great deal of thought to the moment he'd see Ana again, he hadn't considered how Aidrik might respond. He did, after all, love Ana too. And Finn was not here simply to say hello.

But Aidrik embraced him as a brother, and even offered him, and his traveling companions, some spit-roasted lamb for supper. Finn accepted and chewed the tender meat ravenously, eating like a man who'd lifted a tremendous weight off his shoulders.

All the while, Ana watched him. He saw the same look in her eyes as when she'd left, only magnified. *She loves me. Now that it's confirmed, my relief wants to fade to anger, but I can't let it. If we're to have any kind of future together, I can never hold this over her head.*

He couldn't stop watching her. Each moment that passed, her face seemed to blossom with more color. Her pallor was all but gone. She was still thin—ungodly thin, and it killed Finn to see it—but some of the life was returning to her and it gave him hope. He forced his gaze not to travel south. Though he was overjoyed to meet his son soon, the vision of him protruding almost grotesquely from his mother's womb also filled Finn with very conflicted feelings of anger. This could kill her. *Aidrik can heal her. Even if she can't heal herself. He'll be with her through this. And if he can't, no one can.*

"You came swiftly," Aidrik said with a lift of one eyebrow. "I only sent the vision yesterday."

"I didn't need a vision to tell me Ana needed me," Finn replied, more defensively than he intended. A heat rose to his face as he tried to bite back the instinctive alpha male. Finn reminded himself not to stare overlong at the unique scar that sat at Aidrik's temple, in the rough shape of a phoenix. Nor could he dwell on the thought of this man being intimate with his Ana. *You've already accepted it. Now put it away.*

Ana buried a drowsy smile in her cup of warm water.

"She does need you," Aidrik agreed. "I see it now."

"How much longer does she have?" Anne asked, nodding at Ana's belly. "She looks ready to burst."

A cloud passed over Aidrik's gaze. Finn's heart dropped at the sight of it. "Not long. A fortnight, perhaps."

"We need to start preparing, then!" Anne exclaimed, but the tone of the room was somber, reflective. There were more important matters to be discussed first.

"Since you haven't yet revealed your main order of business, allow me to broach the subject," Aidrik continued. Tristan and Anne exchanged fearful glances.

"Fear not, Children of Men. I am not going to crush your optimisms. Least, not today." With the last, Aidrik's eye twinkled, and Finn realized he was attempting a joke.

"Ana's son," Finn began. "*Our* son needs to be born in wedlock in order for him to be a valid heir. Ana and I..."

"Need to be joined in a legally binding marriage," Aidrik finished. "Yes, a pointless tradition, but one Men embrace."

Ana's face registered her surprise at this. There was a spreading darkness in her gaze as her eyes narrowed, distrustfully. *Please don't let her think I'm here just about the estate.*

"That's why you're here?" she asked. Now, her face was inexpressive. Ana was masterful at hiding her emotions once she became aware of them. Finn wished more than anything he could have approached this with her privately. He never intended to do it in front of everyone.

"I would have come either way," Finn was quick to clarify. He tried to send her warm, reassuring thoughts, but it was no use; he could only communicate telepathically when a telepath initiated it. He was not a Deschanel. "I decided on my own I would come for you. I was trying to figure out how, when this came up."

Ana said nothing to this, and Finn's heart sank further.

"It is Anasofiya's choice," Aidrik replied. "But you'll meet no resistance from me."

Of course not. The man thought marriage was silly. A piece of paper would be no inconvenience to him.

"I suppose this is the right thing to do, for Aleksandr's sake." The hurt in her voice was crushing. But beneath that hurt, Finn sensed something more, which he couldn't yet pinpoint. Whatever it was, it seemed to be what kept her emotions shuttered.

"You have no idea what Finn has gone through since you left!" Anne cried, standing defiantly. Finn shook his head at her, signaling her to relent, but she didn't notice, or didn't care. "You broke his heart!"

"Anne," Tristan warned, too late.

"Tristan, it's okay," Ana said steadily, still protecting whatever else she was feeling. "She's right."

"He should hate you, but he doesn't," Anne spat, through clenched teeth, ignoring the glares from Tristan and Finn. "You don't deserve his love."

Before Finn could say a word in defense, Ana turned toward her younger cousin, and flashed her a weary smile. "Anne, I've spent far too many years of my life worrying about the things I did and didn't deserve. Whatever happened between Finn and me, quite frankly, is between us, and I only need to answer to him for my crimes. Not you."

Anne's jaw went slack, speechless.

Finn thought he might lose all hope of success if what he said next was not very carefully constructed.

He knelt before Ana, the stone cold and unforgiving under his knees. He hated that he was surrounded by others in this intimate moment, but waiting any longer might do untold, irreparable damage. "Ana," he said, taking her hands in his. She looked up at him with bleary eyes. "I'm not here for a piece of paper. I'm here because I love you. Despite all that's happened... hell, maybe because of it... I'm still here and I still want to marry you. More than I did when I proposed in Maine, which I know you thought was crazy, but sometimes you just *know,* Ana, and I knew. And yes, this arrangement benefits our son. And that would alone be reason enough to do it. But it isn't why I'm here."

Ana choked back a sob. It was murder to see her like this, dissolving before his eyes.

"I'm also not here to take you away from Aidrik. I think I understand this... evigbond. I don't like it, but I understand it, and I can't change it."

"I don't even understand it," Ana admitted, with a small smile.

Finn looked anxiously at Aidrik. He entirely avoided the eyes of Anne and Tristan, who had no idea what he was about to say next or they might not have agreed to come.

"There's a lot about the last few months of my life that turns everything I believed to be normal on its head. But being around you, and your very peculiar family, has opened my eyes to the idea that our reality... our *norm,* isn't always what everyone else thinks it should be. I can't do anything about what you have with Aidrik. I know he's taken good care of you." At this, Aidrik gave him a tight, but amiable, grin. "But I know you love me, too." Finn paused, and studied Ana, searchingly. "You do love me, right?"

Ana nodded, as the tears streaked down her face, cutting glistening paths down her flushed cheeks. He watched her fight to regain control of herself, and even that, the battle over her emotions, was endearing. "More than I could ever tell you," she replied.

Finn gathered the courage to say the next words. He knew what he was going to propose was crazy, but he'd meditated on it a great deal. It was insane only if you put stock in what others thought. Finn never had. "Don't choose. You can have us both."

Anne made a series of noises expressing her shock and displeasure. Tristan burst into laughter.

"Ana, this motherfucker just offered you a *threesome!*" Tristan cawed, one hand bracing himself against the grime-covered wall.

Aidrik and Ana were both silent.

"Say something," Finn pleaded, after an agonizing silence. "Anything."

Ana looked to Aidrik, who nodded, indicating he supported her decision. "That is... unbelievably generous of you, Finn. But I can't accept," she said finally. "I love you enough I believe you deserve someone who can give you all of herself. You shouldn't have to compromise."

"Finally, you and I see eye to eye on something," Anne snarked from the sidelines.

Finn shot a silencing glance at Anne. "I'm choosing this. I think..." The words failed him.

"It's worth considering," Aidrik joined in, breaking his silence. "I sense no future regret in Finn's offer. He did not come to this decision lightly. He will not later resent you, if you accept."

How Aidrik knew that, Finn could not guess.

"Give us a moment alone," Finn requested. When everyone exchanged glances but didn't move, he added, *"Please."*

It was Aidrik who ushered the others out. When he and Ana were alone, Finn kissed her. He'd inherited, from his father, an inadequacy at finding the right words, but an innate skill in showing what he struggled to articulate.

Ana sat back and drew in a deep breath, but as she went to let it out, the sigh turned to sobs, and the sobs to gasps. He moved as if to take her into his arms, as he once would have, but stopped.

A conversation he had with Nicolas several weeks ago popped into his head.

It's my fucking fault, you know. For how she is, Nicolas had said. The liquor had been hot on his breath, the shame burning equally warm against his face. *I loved her too much. Coddled her. Instead of slapping some sense into her, I encouraged this foolish idea she was broken.*

Finn didn't expect anything he said would help with Nicolas in such a state, so he'd simply said, *She was lucky to have someone who was always there for her.*

No, Nicolas rebutted with laugh so bitter it struck Finn with chills. *I held her back. I was the only one who embraced her as she was. Instead of encouraging her to grow, I fucking stifled her, because I was afraid of losing her, or afraid she'd somehow see what a damn fraud I was.*

I don't understand.

Yes, you do. You know her even better than I do, Nicolas insisted. *And you know damn well she doesn't need a fucking hug and a pat on the back. She needs the truth. She needs people who will tell her when she fucks up, and make her accountable for it! I never could. All I ever gave her was a gilded cage.*

As Ana cried silently before him, Finn watched her, thinking of Nicolas' drunken advice. There were things he needed to say before they could go any further. Things she needed to hear.

"You fucking broke my heart, Ana. Ripped it right out of my chest and discarded it, like it was nothing to you."

"Finn—"

"Like I was just another goddamn mistake of yours! Do you know how that makes me feel? I wasn't even good enough to be put in my own category? You thought I was no different than the random men you fucked back home, and forgot about?"

She stopped crying and looked up, stunned. Her mouth opened, then closed, as she clearly struggled to decide whether there were any words adequate for such a reprisal.

"I wanted to hate you," he said, only recognizing how true this was as the words left his lips. "It would have been a hell of a lot easier if I could have."

"I wouldn't have blamed you for it," Ana said, in a voice so quiet he could hardly hear. "Sometimes I hated myself."

Careful. This isn't why you are here. You've said your piece. "Dammit Ana, even on my worst days, I loved you. And I felt so sure you loved me, too. I understood you had your reasons, even if they made no sense to me. So I forgive you. And I want you to forgive yourself, too."

Once the words were off his chest, he knew the necessity of saying them was more for him than her. Releasing the words allowed whatever bad feelings he harbored toward her to slip away.

"Thank you," she whispered.

"I'm not the boy you left behind, you know," Finn said, pulling his hands down over his face. "I thought all these things you tortured yourself over didn't matter, and I could help you see that. But they do matter. I have a darkness inside of me, too, and it's bigger than you think. Maybe bigger than yours. I'm not afraid of you, Ana. I need you to stop acting like I should be."

She leaned back against the wall, watching him. "I can see the changes in you. And you're right. About all of it," she agreed. "There are a lot of things I understand now that I didn't before."

"And I am *not* compromising," he protested, reaching for her hands, as he pressed them between his. They radiated with heat, and he was struck again with how she had changed. "No, I never imagined I'd be sharing you, and that isn't what I'd hoped for, but there are a dozen other bigger, much bigger, things happening requiring us to be flexible. I've thought about this for months, Ana. I know you need him. Hell, I'm glad you *have* him because I don't know if we could figure things out without him. He knows how to keep our son, and you, safe. But I know you need me, too."

Ana looked down and away, then took a deep breath and met his gaze. "Leaving you was the hardest thing I've ever done. It was also the most regret I've ever felt, though I don't know that I had any other choice."

"No," he agreed reluctantly. "You didn't. And I see that now."

"I've never seen myself as the marrying type, Finn. Not ever. But the thought of being your wife fills me with..." She then placed a trembling hand over her swollen belly and sighed. "I still can't even believe you're here."

"I said I would follow you anywhere. And I would wait forever. You're it for me, Ana. You're the only one until now, and you'll be the only one after, even if you turn me away."

"I'll never turn you away again," Ana promised, as she slipped her hands from between his, and pressed his folded ones over her heart. "You weren't the only one who's been making plans. There's so much I know now... too much to go into at this very emotional moment," she said, laughing, "but know I love you and I will never, ever walk away from you like I did in Louisiana. The girl I left behind couldn't give you what you deserved. Even if I had to do it all over again, I think it would have ended with me leaving. But the woman I am now... the one I've allowed myself to become... well, she's capable of a whole lot more."

Finn saw in Ana's expression evidence of the things she

always felt herself incapable of. Above all, he saw the inexorable love radiating off her.

She opened her mouth to speak again, but in one quick, desperate motion she instead threw her arms around Finn's neck and kissed him. This was not the ardent, disconnected kisses Ana had been giving away freely for years. This was the gentle, passion of someone who has an ocean of words to say and can only set them free by choosing a subtle, more intimate path.

"My offer is sincere," he said, after their kisses faded to tender cuddling. He pressed his forehead gently to hers. "It isn't a compromise, to love you, and also know you and our son will always be safe."

"Then yes," she whispered, through tears and kisses.

"One thing," Finn said, shoving down his joy and relief in order to get out this one, last important order of business. "I love all of you, even the darkness. I know who you are. But I can't live in fear of wondering if I'm going to wake up one day and you'll be gone. If you want to yell, scream, kick, bite, cry, I can deal with any of that. Throw it all at me, Ana, I can take it. But we won't survive you leaving again."

"We understand one another now," she assured him, as she wound her fingers through his. She said nothing else, but Finn saw in her eyes, reflected back at him, all of the things he had hoped to find at the end of his journey.

16- ANNE

Anne went in search of flowers, having it in mind to make her cousin a hair wreath for her nuptials. But she also needed the time alone, to think.

The last of her hope, that Finn might come around, fled as soon as Anne saw Ana throw herself into Finn's arms, sobbing with regret and powerful love. Anne's own iciness for her cousin began to melt as she reminded herself everyone had regrets. Anne could think of a few of her own. The death of her mother sat at the front of that list, a constant reminder.

But Anne was astounded by Finn's proposal to Ana and Aidrik. She thought him foolish, and so blindly in love that he was throwing any solution he thought might stick. Part of her remained indignantly convinced he would come to regret this decision in the not-too-distant future, and it would serve him right for being so irrational.

And yet... Anne knew better. This was a man who'd spent months down at the river, formulating his plan. No, Finn knew exactly what he was getting himself into and, somehow, not only accepted it, but embraced it.

She paused, glancing back at the old castle, as an unexpected sadness coursed through her. She supposed she always knew Finn was not The One. But it had been nice, for a while, to think he might be.

Anne overheard Finn the afternoon before, as he whispered the contents of his heart to his beloved Ana. *Sometimes, I don't even know where I stop and you begin,* he had said.

It was the kind of thought that stopped you in your tracks. Anne could not even *begin* to fathom the enormity of his feelings. No man had ever taken a significant interest in her who didn't harbor the expectation she might lift her skirt, as many of the other bayou girls did so eagerly. But they were always supremely disappointed when she would turn them away after a bit of heavy petting. Ah, the names she'd been called! Certainly she'd never been accused of being so close to someone they couldn't determine where they ended and she began.

And if someone ever did say those words to her, it wouldn't be Finn.

Somehow, that was okay.

She'd survived worse.

Anne shivered as she trudged through the snow. Though it was spring, it was an unusually *cold* spring, and many of the flowers were hiding or buried. At last, she spotted a thicket of beautiful white blooms and knelt to pick them.

"These will do quite nicely," she said, with a pleased smile.

"God must be pleased," Tristan said, as they gathered in the morning for the small ceremony. He gestured toward the beautiful, clear sky. Not a cloud in sight.

"I thought you didn't believe in God," Anne questioned, eyeing him uncertainly.

Tristan chuckled, twisting his lips together. His wayward, chocolate hair blew rebelliously in the breeze. "Christ, woman! Of course I believe in God! I said the Deschanels were a lot of failed Catholics who God would smite down if we dared cross his consecrated grounds. But we're not *complete* heathens!"

Though Tristan was an acquired taste, Anne had to admit to herself that he had a charm to him.

Anne had spent the last hour helping Ana prepare for her wedding. Her older cousin had been stunned speechless when Anne pulled out the beautiful white dress Colleen had made just for her, for this occasion, packed carefully with tissue in a duffle all its own. It had a low collar but long sleeves, bedecked in ornate lace from top to bottom, with the midsection let out to allow room. Anne thought her cousin looked like a Celtic princess, with her porcelain complexion and lovely red hair falling down over the white lace in loose waves. As Anne placed the crown of white blossoms on Ana's head, a small sigh escaped her lips.

She could almost overlook the dark bags under her cousin's tired, sick eyes, and the looming fear that in a couple of weeks she may go into labor and never come out of it. *No, you musn't think that, not ever. You know what happened last time you conjured up images of loved ones dying.* Yes, she remembered all too well the sight of foliage coming through the hospital windows to strangle her mother. She hadn't wanted that, not really. But her abilities often reached deep into the dark recesses of her subconscious, pulling out desires she did not even know she had. And who was to say, deep down, she might still hate her cousin and wish her harm?

Anne filled her head instead with the lovely, angelic image of her glowing and happy cousin, and of the joy she would feel when she walked out on to the moor and met her soul mate in the holiest of vows.

"Thank you," Ana said with a breathless sigh, as she observed herself in the small compact mirror Anne handed her. "I haven't seen my own reflection, other than in the water, in months. I thought I might see a horrible monster staring back to me."

"You're not a monster," Anne assured, picking up on Ana's double meaning. "Or if you are, you might be the prettiest monster I've ever seen."

Ana smiled then, looking down at her swollen hands. "Thank you for taking care of Finn."

Anne gazed down at her cousin in stunned silence, followed by an immediate, quiet shame. Had Ana read her thoughts somehow?

"Tristan told me about your friendship and affection for him," Ana revealed, solving the mystery. "It should have been me. But it will be, from now on."

Anne nodded, swallowing nervously. She had never taken compliments very well. "Let's go meet your groom."

As they stepped out into the brisk morning air, Tristan waited with a purposeful grin on his face. He held out one arm to Ana, and Anne retained the other. Together, they guided their cousin as they stepped through the ruins of Gwynfryn, and up to the hill where Finn and Aidrik awaited.

Some of the snow had melted overnight. Smaller, more melodic birds than the pigeons and rooks were singing and flying overhead, to and fro. Anne thought, had the circumstances not been so staid, it was a beautiful day for a wedding.

At the top of the hill, Aidrik and Finn stood, under the large branches of a very old weeping willow. When Finn saw Ana, his knees buckled slightly but he quickly righted himself, standing straighter.

As they ascended the hill, Aidrik moved down to take the place of Anne and Tristan. "Is there not also a tradition requiring someone to give away the bride?" he asked, with a near imperceptible smile. "Aye, well I shall do it."

Very symbolic, Anne thought. In a lot of ways, Aidrik did seem a father figure to Ana, guiding her through this new life, placed on her shoulders when Aidrik gave her the Sveising. He was Ana's divine love, while Finn was the man who held her heart. *What I would do for even one man to look at me the way these two men look at her.*

"You are radiant, *Kjære*," Aidrik whispered with uncommon tenderness, as he snaked his strong arm under her, steadying her as she struggled up the hill.

Ana leaned slightly more into him, smiling, but her eyes were fixed on Finn's waiting, outstretched hand.

As they reached the top, Tristan took his place next to Finn, Aidrik next to Ana, and Anne before them. She took one look down into the sparkling bay, then again at the happy couple, and decided the day was perfect.

It had been years since she last performed this ceremony, but the words came to her effortlessly as she introduced the couple, and their intentions.

When at last it came to the vows, Anne started to instruct them, but Finn put up a polite, interrupting hand. "We have our own," he said, his eyes never leaving Ana.

Anne blushed, nodding at him. "Go ahead."

The beaming smile on Finn's face couldn't hide his shaking voice, and hands, as he said, "I, Finnegan James St. Andrews, son of Andrew and Claire, will love you, Anasofiya Aleksandrovna Vasilyeva Deschanel until the end of time. I will protect you, keep you safe, and face every obstacle with you in my heart, and by my side. I am yours. Forever."

Tears streamed down Ana's face as he placed the ring on her trembling hands. Her eyes followed every movement. "This is *my* evigbond," he said, for her ears only.

Ana wiped the tears with the back of her hand, then took a deep breath, smiling even brighter than Finn. "I, Anasofiya Aleksandrovna Vasilyeva Deschanel, daughter of Augustus and Ekatherina, will love you, Finnegan James St. Andrews, until the end of time. I will protect you, keep you safe, and face every obstacle with you in my heart, and by my side. I am yours. Forever."

Tristan handed Ana a ring then, and she drew in a steadying breath as she slid it onto Finn's sturdy hand. "This is *my* evig-bond," she whispered.

Anne concluded by pronouncing them man and wife, but they were already locked in embrace, kissing through their tears of joy.

When at last they withdrew, Aidrik kissed both Finn and Ana's foreheads, blessing the union, "The threads of fate weave slowly, until at last, an unbreakable knot."

Then, Aidrik asked if Anne and Tristan might give him a moment alone with the newly wedded couple, so he might present his wedding gift.

17- FINN

Finn had a brief moment of panic as Anne and Tristan descended the hill, wondering how literally Aidrik had taken him when he suggested they share Ana. But his fears were quickly allayed, as Aidrik was never one to prolong suspense.

"Anasofiya will live many years," Aidrik began, facing Finn. "I don't know how many. Her Empyrean blood far outweighs her blood of Man now, after the Sveising. As it is now, your life will end, long before hers."

"Thank you for that depressing reminder on our wedding day," Finn muttered.

"While I am fond of you, and would mourn your passing, it will destroy Anasofiya," Aidrik continued, ignoring him. "I seek to prevent that."

"I'm not leaving her, if that's what you're suggesting," Finn professed, lacing his fingers through Ana's. "Ever."

Ana said nothing. She watched Aidrik with slowly widening eyes.

"It is not. I am offering you Sveising."

Finn was entirely shocked at this. While he'd considered

there would come a day when he would fade to dust and Ana would live on, he'd seen it as an inevitable conclusion. It hadn't occurred to him there could be a solution.

"It is unpredictable in humans. Possibly, it will surface abilities you previously could not access. Ideally, it will also grant you a lifespan equivalent to Anasofiya's."

"But—" Finn fumbled through his long list of questions, unable to decide on one.

"It doesn't hurt," Ana whispered reassuringly, squeezing his hand.

When Finn turned to face her, he once again had tears in his eyes. "Silly girl," he scolded, in a choked voice, "that's not what I'm worried about."

"Then what?" she asked. Unlike the day before, where the unknown realm of his thoughts had panicked her, she was calm, and simply listening.

"I don't want to lose any part of me," he attempted to explain. He reminded himself to lessen his grip on her hands, lest he crush them. "After Aidrik gave you the Sveising, you..." He let that last end there. It would do no good for the small, insecure side of him to add: *...you stopped needing me.*

Ana pressed her head against his chest then, and he was reminded of the winter mornings in Maine when she'd sleep, nude, against him, using his body as heat. The comforting sensation of her tiny breath against his skin; the rise and fall of her chest as her breasts pressed into his side. Her hair falling every which way, covering him in a protective blanket. *This is love,* he would think. *This right here.*

"The Sveising only made me love you more, Finn. Enough that I couldn't put you in danger," she assured him.

"Aye," Aidrik added. "If anything, it will strengthen the bond. Between all three of us."

Finn knew he faced an enormous decision. The biggest of

his life. If he accepted, he might live hundreds, or even thousands, of years. And he would do it by Ana and Aidrik's side.

He wouldn't inevitably slow down, grow weary, and perish. He would remain twenty-seven, always. Finn had always thought eighty would be a very nice age to die. Enough living behind you, and a wonderful rest ahead.

But if he said no, Ana would be forced to watch him die in another fifty years or so. And she would carry that grief with her all her long days. *We won't survive you leaving again,* he'd said to her. But what of him, leaving her?

And then there was Aleksandr, his son, to think about. Aleksandr, who shared the blood of all three of them. His son would need him, too.

"Do it," Finn decided. Ana pressed into him harder, and he felt both her heart beat faster as well as the soft thumping of his son kicking. *This is love. This right here.*

Aidrik instructed him to close his eyes. As he did, he felt Aidrik's warm fingers against his temple, and a hot, tingly sensation ran the length of his entire body, as he felt it change, rapidly. While his limbs shivered with life, Finn was flooded with all the memories, experiences, and knowledge of the four-thousand-year-old being standing before him. His spiritual father, and partner. The central tie binding their new family together.

When it was over, Ana stood before him and he still loved her with all his heart.

"More," Finn declared, watching his wife smiling up at him, as he placed both hands against her belly, and their son within. "I love you more."

18- TRISTAN

Aidrik treated them to the rest of the lamb for the wedding feast. Tristan, who'd been raised in the Upper Garden District with all luxuries afforded to him, had never eaten food made out in the wild before, but he thought the succulent lamb was the tastiest thing he'd ever consumed.

He watched the small wedding party as they joked and laughed, a far cry from the mood only a day ago. Anne was even smiling and enjoying the merriment, and Ana was the happiest Tristan had ever seen her. Finn, after a great deal of whiskey, sang Irish drinking songs, dancing around the fire.

It was done. They'd succeeded. They found Ana, Finn married her, and despite the road ahead, all was well for now.

But the reunion had not been the only success. Tristan himself felt different after these days away; stronger, or perhaps simply more in tune with who he really was, and wanted to be. He didn't quite understand the tether his mother had attached to him until he'd broken from it. And with some distance between them, he only wanted to grow further into himself, and these realizations.

Once I graduate college next month, I'll offer my services to Mercy and Nicolas, he decided, the certainty of his path growing with each passing thought.

Tristan reached out through his thoughts, through the many stars in his mind's sky, and found Aunt Colleen again.

Tristan! We're all eager for the news. Please tell us it's good.

Weeeelllll... Tristan teased, realizing he wielded a small, but important power with this information he had and they did not. Then he smiled, caught up in the mood around him. *We have a very happy, very married couple here.*

Oh, splendid news! Everyone will be thrilled to hear it. Nicolas especially. He has been going mad with worry.

Good, he can be a bit of an ass sometimes.

And the paperwork is signed? Ana understands she must keep her name?

Yes, but she took his name anyway, and put it somewhere in the middle of her long list of crazy Russian names. Here, let me look. Tristan pulled the paper from his inner jacket pocket. *Ahh, yes. Anasofiya Aleksandrovna Vasilyeva St. Andrews Deschanel. I mean, is she for real with this shit?*

I think it's lovely, Aunt Colleen sent back. *In fact, it's perfect.*

Whatever. Anyway, we will be back after the baby is born—

No! Aunt Colleen responded, so loudly his head pounded. *You must return immediately. We need the paperwork filed before Ana gives birth.*

But I thought Anne was going to be her midwife?

Yes, we thought so, too, but the Sullivans insist we must have the documentation and it is far too risky for you to mail it.

Tristan looked around at the celebratory bunch and felt a small surge of sadness. The happiness in this ancient, musty room was greater than any he'd felt at his welcoming home in all his life. He was not quite ready to leave it. Even Anne was growing on him.

As if reading his mind, Anne leaned in and winked. "Tell Aunt Colleen I said hi."

Your protégé sends her regards.

Be kind to Anne. This was a difficult journey for her, in many ways.

Yes, Tristan knew that. At first, he'd found her unreciprocated pining for Finn foolish and obnoxious, but he saw now his cousin had the strong, powerful heart of a Deschanel. Loyal and unfailing, until the end. They couldn't help who they were.

Tristan? Are you still there?

Have the attorneys arrange for our travel tomorrow night. I'll make sure we're back in Cardiff by early evening, Tristan responded finally.

Two tickets? Or three?

Two, Tristan replied, as he watched Finn and Ana, cuddling near the fire, glowing in each other's presence. *This mission was very successful. Finn and Aidrik are all Ana needs. I'll bring the paperwork, and Anne, home with me.*

19- FINN

Tristan had been carefully observing Finn's driving, so it only took a few pointers, some practice with the stick-shift, before he felt confident in his ability to get himself and Anne to the airport. As the rental car faded into the mid-morning fog, the events of the prior day began to feel even more real to Finn. *This is my home now. Wherever she is.*

He thought of his brother, Jon, back in Maine. They hadn't parted on good terms. Before Finn and Ana were a couple, Ana and Jon had a brief liaison. When Ana chose Finn, Jon punished her with cruel silences and cutting remarks, and eventually those gestures turned darker, culminating in an attack. This incident drove an irreparable wedge between the brothers, but had also been the catalyst for Ana's attempt to take her own life.

Finn could feel, as Ana told him he would, the energy and life coursing through his veins now. He felt as if he could run fifty miles without taking a breath. That he could swim across the Atlantic. He didn't know how long he would live, but he knew it would be far longer than Jon. Before Jon passed, they would need to find their peace.

But not yet.

Many unknowns lay ahead. Soon, Aleksandr would be born into the world, and Finn prayed Aidrik was strong enough to bring Ana through it. Once Aleksandr was here, they would need to start plans to meet with the rebels and figure out how to bring down the Eldre Senetat. Aidrik was convinced Agripin, son and heir of Emperor Aeron, was a secret sympathizer. His plan centered around using Agripin to stir the hearts of the rebels.

But that was all too much to think about right now. Finn wanted to enjoy these days with Ana, before the world went insane.

Aidrik had given Ana and Finn privacy on their wedding night, but Finn hadn't even thought of more than holding her, despite how badly he might want to consummate their union. Though she'd thrown herself into his arms when he found her, that strength came from a rush of adrenaline. She couldn't even make it up the hill alone on her wedding day. Amidst all the emotion of the reunion, and subsequent wedding, he couldn't forget her perilous physical situation.

Instead, he gently peeled the clothes from her, then removed his own. "Come here, pretty girl," he invited, opening his arms. She smiled, understanding. Her warm face fell against his chest, and her arms twined around him, brushing his neck with her fingers. He pulled her in, protectively, caressing her lower back as the fire burned hot nearby.

They were simply Finn and Ana again, as they had been, on the shores of Maine. But now, it was more, though Finn struggled to define it beyond the way his heart finally felt whole, and his soul forged with purpose.

As anticipated, the Sveising enhanced Finn's natural connection to weather and nature. But he was now also something of an empath. Not a strong one, but he felt very keenly the contentment and peace radiating from his wife. This was new, and it was wonderful. Before, he'd always sensed she had one foot out the door. Now, she had both of those beautiful feet twined through his legs.

Finn was no longer afraid.

"Are you happy?" he asked, knowing the answer, but wanting to hear her say it, again.

"Oh, yes," she whispered, her hot breath tickling his chest, as her finger traced his torso slowly, hovering above his waist. "I don't know that I ever understood what happiness felt like, before now. Or how badly I wanted it."

"I'll protect you," Finn vowed, placing a hand over the one she had against his heart. He could feel both their heartbeats, through her hand. "Whatever comes."

"We'll protect each other," Ana amended. She struggled to rise and then ran her lips down the long scar which ran from his chest to his midsection. A reminder he had limitations. And he had others to think about now. There was no room for recklessness, where they were going.

"Even when the whole world falls apart around us, nothing will change. We will be okay," he vowed, lifting her face back up toward his. "You and me, *Mo Shíorghrá*."

"What does that mean?" Ana asked.

"'My eternal love,'" Finn answered. "I heard my grandfather say it once, to my grandma."

"This *is* love, Finn," she replied, with a tiny, contended sigh. Her hands twisted around his, Ana pillowed her head on Finn's shoulder so her distended belly was tucked snugly against him, connecting all three of their hearts. "This right here."

"It is, isn't it?" Finn agreed, his hand protectively over his child, smiling as his wife pressed her lips against his swiftly beating heart.

The Deschanel Curse is back, and the entire family assembles when beloved family members fall victim. But is there anything they can actually do to stop it from claiming even more of their loved ones?

Don't miss a minute. Download ***Midnight Dynasty*** today.

WANT A GLIMPSE INTO ELIZABETH'S VISIONS? READ FURTHER FOR AN EXCERPT.

MIDNIGHT DYNASTY EXCERPT

ELIZABETH

Elizabeth woke abruptly, sweat pooling at her brow. Her dreams only grew to levels this vivid when their reality was imminent.

Beside her, Connor lay snoring, undisturbed. He had never, not in nearly three decades of marriage, had trouble sleeping through his wife's episodes. She could wake screaming at the top of her lungs and he'd continue on in uninterrupted, restful bliss.

As a seer, Elizabeth often saw glimpses of the future. When awake, her visions were unreliable. She was only given snippets, with much of what she saw open to interpretation. When dreaming, however, they were painfully lucid. She could see the future in all its terror or glory, with no filter to help ease the burden.

Of course, as a Deschanel, this ability was not wholly unique. Her relatives were healers, empaths, and other powerfully "gifted" individuals. But the rest of them experienced things *in the now*. They laid their hands on someone sick and that person was healed. They sensed disquiet in another and helped soothe it. Elizabeth only ever saw what was to come. And, whether it came to her in a dream or otherwise, it always, without fail, came to pass.

She glanced at the clock: two in the morning. Connor would be waking in a few hours to head in to the law firm. Tristan, her son, would be dead to the world until lunchtime.

Though Tristan didn't figure into her dream—thank God, she couldn't lose another child to this wretched Curse—she still had a pressing urge to check on him. Since he was born, nearly twenty-one years ago to the day, she'd always feared he would stop breathing in his sleep. Some nights, even now, she sat at his bedside and watched his chest rise and fall. She'd done the same thing for Danielle too, but now Danielle was gone.

This was the life Elizabeth Sullivan led day in and day out: one of dread. Fear the Deschanel Curse would continue to strike those she loved. Terror it might take Tristan, as it had Danielle.

Tristan lay askew in his old childhood bed, long legs dangling out from the side of his sheets. Elizabeth released the sigh she'd been holding in, and sat quietly on the pine chest beside his bed. Once filled with toys and plush friends, now it lay stuffed with forgotten sports gear and a messy stack of dog-eared video game magazines.

He wasn't in the vision. He was safe, she kept telling herself. But years later, she was still unable to get the sight of her only daughter, lying broken in the street, out of her head. Eyes open, closed, it didn't matter. That image was burned in her heart and mind for all of time. It was a wound that would never heal, a grief she would never recover from.

Though Tristan was safe, for now, there were others in the family, people she loved, who were not. Nieces and nephews she watched grow up. Children who never would.

And there was nothing—not one thing—Elizabeth could do to stop it. It was going to happen. The only unknown was *when*.

Pick up your copy of *Midnight Dynasty* now, and have it ready to curl up at your next reading session!

ALSO BY SARAH M. CRADIT

THE SAGA OF CRIMSON & CLOVER

The House of Crimson and Clover Series

The Storm and the Darkness

Shattered

The Illusions of Eventide

Bound

Midnight Dynasty

Asunder

Empire of Shadows

Myths of Midwinter

The Hinterland Veil

The Secrets Amongst the Cypress

Within the Garden of Twilight

House of Dusk, House of Dawn

Midnight Dynasty Series

A Tempest of Discovery

A Storm of Revelations

The Seven Series

1970

1972

1973

1974

1975

1976

1980

~

Vampires of the Merovingi Series

The Island

~

Crimson & Clover Lagniappes (Bonus Stories)

Lagniappes are standalone stories that can be read in any order.

St. Charles at Dusk: The Story of Oz and Adrienne

Flourish: The Story of Anne Fontaine

Surrender: The Story of Oz and Ana

Shame: The Story of Jonathan St. Andrews

Fire & Ice: The Story of Remy & Fleur

Dark Blessing: The Landry Triplets

Pandora's Box: The Story of Jasper & Pandora

The Menagerie: Oriana's Den of Iniquities

A Band of Heather: The Story of Colleen and Noah

The Ephemeral: The Story of Autumn & Gabriel

Banshee: The Story of Giselle Deschanel

For more information, and exciting bonus material, visit www.

sarahmcradit.com

ABOUT THE AUTHOR

~

Sarah is the *USA Today* Bestselling Author of the Paranormal Southern Gothic world, The Saga of Crimson & Clover, born of her combined passion for New Orleans, and the mysterious complexity of human nature. Her work has been described as rich, emotive, and highly dimensional.

An unabashed geek, Sarah enjoys studying obscure subjects like the Plantagenet and Ptolemaic dynasties, and settling debates on provocative Tolkien topics such as why the Great Eagles are not Gandalf's personal taxi service. Passionate about travel, Sarah has visited over twenty countries collecting sparks of inspiration (though New Orleans is where her heart rests). She's a self-professed expert at crafting original songs to sing to her very patient pets, and a seasoned professional at finding ways to humiliate herself (bonus points if it happens in public). When at home in Oregon, her husband and best friend, James, is very kind about indulging her love of fast German cars and expensive lattes.

www.sarahmcradit.com